Tales From

Russ Crossley Presents Tales From Space

Tales From Space

Tales From Space

Russ Crossley Presents: Tales From Space

Published by 53rd Street Publishing

Copyright 2012 Russ Crossley

Cover image © Michael Knight | Dreamstime.co

Tales From Space

Table of Contents

Introduction

Countdown

T.I.N. Men

The Secret

The Family Line

Big Business

About the Author

Other titles by the Author

Tales From Space
Introduction

I'm very pleased to offer you a collection of space related stories. I have been a fan of science fiction since I was a child watching the Mercury, Gemini, and Apollo space programs in the 1960's. I began, like most children, reading comic books mostly related to science fiction.

Super heroes, UFO's, aliens, anything that smacked of science fiction I would read it. And any movie or television show with science fiction elements were my staple of entertainment viewing, and believe me the special effects weren't what they are today.

What was common about science fiction stories then was the stories often had uplifting endings and the good guys won. They always won. Or if they didn't win the story told how they survived their terrible circumstances. Don't misunderstand me I really love science fiction today, even without endings where the hero clearly wins.

I hope you enjoy this collection of my tales from space and hope they will become your favorites as they are mine.

In the collection you will find stories with impossible odds, satire where the fast food companies run the galaxy, AI robots locked in a civil war, and space travelers with very human problems.

Feel free to contact me on twitter or facebook. I'd love to hear from you.

Russ Crossley
March 2012

Tales From Space

Tales From Space

Countdown

Elvis Pepper sat on his bunk staring at the image on the monitor on his desk. His eyes brimmed with tears and his mind was having trouble processing what he was seeing.

When the asteroid the size of Texas struck the Earth in the Atlantic ocean it vaporized that ocean and hurled a huge cloud of dust and debris high into the atmosphere. The clouds of superheated air quickly formed a shroud around the Earth and winds spread a wave of destruction at speeds of over two hundred and fifty miles an hour outward in waves from the epicenter where the asteroid struck.

The surveillance satellite watching the catastrophe was stationed within range of the electromagnetic pulse so as expected within a few minutes of impact the satellite's transmission feed was lost.

As the screen changed to white fuzz a tear escaped Elvis' right eye and travelled down his cheek. In the next few hours everything humanity had built over the last ten thousand years would be scoured from the surface of the planet by a force greater than the collective power of every atomic weapon ever constructed. Nature had provided a far more lethal end for the Earth than mankind ever could.

The four orbiting Lagrange stations in Earth orbit, and the fifth at L2 position on the other side of the moon, would keep the dream of humanity alive. All that remained now of the human race were twenty thousand Adam and Eve's to start over, and hopefully some day re-populate the Earth.

Like a zombie Elvis got up from his bunk and walked to the desk where he fingered the off button on the side of the monitor and it went dark. He let out a slow breath. He'd been preparing for this day for five years yet when the time came the image of such terrible destruction affected him at a far deeper level than he had anticipated.

After he wiped his eyes with the back of his hand then went to the door of his cabin and keyed the code into the keypad in the wall next to the door. There was a barely audible click before the door side aside and he stepped into the corridor.

He passed several cabin doors on his way to the communication center where he was due to relieve Selma Hollings. It had been two hours since impact and they were supposed to keep monitoring communications from the underground bunkers where other survivors were housed, and the other L stations.

Tales From Space

The bunkers were constructed in the twentieth century during the cold war, and now in the middle of the twenty-first century the bunkers were being used to protect a cadre of scientists and other experts that were unsuccessful in the world wide lottery for the twenty thousand coveted positions on the Lagrangian stations, or those deemed ineligible for the lottery due to age or for medical reasons but were still valuable.

Only fertile people between the ages of twelve and forty five were eligible to enter the lottery, but the worlds leading scientists agreed these bunkers would save an additional thirty thousand people. They expected these survivors would be able to hold out in the bunkers for the next five years. Estimates were until the dust and debris thrown into the atmosphere would have settled by then.

But Elvis wasn't worried about the survival of thirty thousand people. He was concerned about the survival of one person. His wife Yvette.

Her PhD in immunization technology made her eligible for the bunker in the Ural mountains after she was deemed unsuitable for the lottery. Her inability to have children made her ineligible to even apply. But her scientific expertise made her indispensible for the future survival in the harsh environment expected in five years.

He told her wouldn't go without her, but he would never have qualified for one of the bunkers. After many long, tearful arguments he agreed to go to the L1 station. They would stay linked by com sat as long as they were able. They would both survive just not together.

Now that he'd witnessed the destruction he knew he'd made the wrong decision.

Tales From Space

I should have stayed with her as long as possible, he thought. But then I'd be dead.

A lump of fear knotted his guts and his heart beat hard in his chest. He grew more anxious with each step as he raced to the communications center. He was one of five specialists responsible to maintain and operate the com systems between the stations. And for the time being with any Earth based survivors.

The stations were shielded against electromagnetic interference so unlike the satellites they would be able to maintain communications.

"I need to stay focused," he muttered as he passed cabin after cabin. The sobs his fellow survivors echoed in the empty corridor and followed him as he rushed along the corridor toward the lift that would take him to the command deck. The captain would need him today so he had to shake off his fear and his uncertainty.

Problem was he wasn't sure he could put aside what remained of his humanity. In fact he wasn't sure any of them could.

The lift doors closed behind him after he entered. Good thing he was alone because he wanted to scream out how unfair all this was. He closed his eyes and sighed.

The end of the world, the separation from his wife, the end of everything he held dear felt like a tremendous weight crushing him under with despair.

He would never feel a warm breeze on his face or witness the sunrise over the purple mountains of his late father's cabin on Seesaw mountain. He'd never swim in the ocean or smell wood smoke from a camp fire. Stars would never twinkle again and his dog would never run in the tall grass behind his uncles barn.

Tales From Space

The doors opened as the lift stopped on the command deck. He opened his eyes and stepped out just before the doors closed behind him.

No one was around, he was alone. He walked to the com panel and touched the power button. The board lit up and the screens came to life. Even though the station was shielded the captain ordered all nonessential systems be powered down until after impact.

The screens flickered then steadied. The external cameras directed at Earth showed the fierce red cloud of energy had spread half way across the United States laying waste to cities, towns, open plains, everything. Every plant, animal and human would be vaporized. No pain, no suffering.

In a way he almost envied them. At least their end would be quick. If the eggheads were correct the debris trailing the asteroid might end this attempt at keeping the human race viable might even before it began. A rocky missile the size of a tennis ball would puncture the station and compromise its atmosphere killing most if not all of the inhabitants in the process.

Elvis felt smaller and more insignificant than he had ever in his life. "Activate holo-assistant," he said as he picked up a com node and placed it in his right ear.

There was a shimmer and Maple appeared next to him. She wore a sad-eyed, sympathetic expression on her holographic features. Dressed in her lab suit and with the glasses perched on the end of her small nose she looked every part the scientist the designer had built into her.

Though Elvis knew her emotions were memory engrams programmed into her matrix he really needed a friend right now. Since Maple had been with him since his training started five years ago she had become just a friend. He smiled to himself as he recalled the memory of Yvette actually getting jealous of the "other woman" in his life.

"Good times," he said quietly.

"I disagree," said Maple in a dulcet tone.

Elvis paused to look at her. "What?"

"Well, sir this is not a good time, as you put it. It is the end of planet Earth as a home for humans."

"Thanks for reminding me," he said sarcastically. He shook his head. "I was recalling one happy memory and you had to ruin it."

Maple's eyes widened. "Sorry, sir. Sometimes I forget my manners."

"Never mind. Contact L3 and see if they can get me an angle of the bunker in the Ural mountains. Or is that too difficult?"

"No, sir right away."

There was a short pause and a familiar voice came through the com node in his ear. "L3, Pumper Jackson speaking'."

"Pump, it's E. I need a link to your cams directed at the Ural bunkers."

"Hey, E. Man, wasn't that impact thingy sumthin?"

"Yeah, Pump it was that." His heart skipped a beat and for a second he thought his next words would catch in his throat. He coughed then managed to say, "Anyway, can you set up the link?"

"Isn't that where Yvette is?"

'Yeah, Pump she's there. And will you boost the signal for me so I can talk to her?"

"I need authorization from—"

"Really, Pump? Really?! It's me, Pump!" He tried to control the anger in his voice but failed. He didn't need a lecture on procedure right now. He needed to talk to his wife before it was too late.

Elvis sighed heavily and his shoulders slumped. "Sorry, Pump. I didn't mean to be short with you. It's just that—" His next words caught at the back of his throat.

"Yeah, okay, E. No problemo. I'll have Lucy establish the link right away." Lucy was Pump's holo-assistant. "Set your monitor to receive."

"It's done, sir," Maple said before he issued the order.

The monitor flickered then steadied and he could see the Ural range untouched, pristine and rugged jutting into the sky.

West of the mountains the edge of the shock wave headed across Europe. It had just wiped away Germany. Millions of people died as he stared at the monitor.

He swallowed hard then said, "L1 to Ural Command, over."

Silence.

"L1 to Ural command," he repeated.

There was a crackle of static then a heavily accented voice responded. "This is Ural Command. Ivan the Terrible speaking. Go ahead L1."

"Ivan!" Elvis smiled to himself. The big man had befriended both he and Yvette during the initial training phase. They had enjoyed dinners and golf games with Ivan and his wife, Simone. Simone won a spot of L2 so Ivan and he had that much in common. "How're things going?"

"EP! How nice to hear your voice, my friend. So far everything is going as planned. We lost contact with the Washington bunkers and the ones in Berlin, Helsinki and Ottawa but they told us that would happen. We're anticipating to reestablish contact twelve hours after the impact wave has dissipated." There was a brief pause. "According to current estimates that should be in two days."

Elvis swiveled in his seat to face Maple. He removed the com node from his ear and wrapped it tight in his fist. He motioned for the hologram to lean closer. "How long until the impact wave reaches the Urals?" he whispered.

"Seventeen minutes," she said.

He nodded then placed the node back in his ear and turned back to face the monitor. "Ivan, I need to speak with Yvette. Can you patch me through?"

"Yes, of course."

There was another pause then his wife's voice came over the node. "E?" she said. He could hear the fear in her voice.

Elvis swallowed hard as his mouth dried. "You okay, my love?"

"Yes. So far," came the reply.

"So far?"

"There have been fifteen suicides reported in the past hour."

No! She couldn't. There was still a chance however small. "How about you?" His voice trembled as he spoke and his heart began to beat faster.

"Don't be concerned, E. Suicide has never been part of my make up."

He heard her swallow and wanted to jump through the com system to wrap her in his arms. "I know, Yvette. It's just up until now this nightmare has been theoretical. The reality is very different. I'm worried what any of us will do."

"Did you see the impact?" she said changing the subject.

"Yes," he whispered. As long as he lived he'd never forget what he'd seen. That terrible image had been burned into his brain permanently.

"The captain has ordered a full briefing in ten minutes," interrupted Maple. "He wants the entire population to meet in the recreation hall."

He looked at Maple and raised both eyebrows. She understood his meaning. They were on a countdown.

"Fourteen minutes," she said softly.

"Advise my section chief I'll be late."

"I don't think—" Elvis silenced the hologram with a glare.

"Yes, sir."

Elvis flushed the sudden burst of anger from his system by rolling his shoulders and expelling a long, deep breath.

"E, are you okay?" asked Yvette.

"Yes, of course. Don't be concerned about me. I'll be right here after the impact wave has passed your bunker. And I'm staying at this post until we reestablish contact. Nothing or no one can budge me. Like I told you when we last saw each other we will never be apart, ever."

"But they could charge you with something. Maybe treason, or worse."

Yvette had always been too sweet for her own good. It was why he loved her so much. But what did any of that matter now? The governments and their laws that had ruled the planet had been swept away like so many dry leaves in the fall. The chances of any of them, or their eventual offspring, surviving was a long shot and they all knew it. Slim as the odds were they had to at least try. The struggle for survival was what made them human.

"Yvette, my darling does any of that matter anymore?"

She laughed half-heartedly. "No, I guess not."

Elvis glanced at Maple. She held up two fingers. Two minutes until contact. He was running out of time.

"Yvette, I want you to know I don't blame you for us not being able to have children. The lab accident wasn't your fault. I never thought that not for one millisecond."

"It's okay, E," she said. "You're just—" A sudden burst of static ion his ear forced him to pull the com node from his ear. He looked at Maple and she nodded and averted her eyes. The wave of superheated air had struck the Ural mountain range knocking out all communications.

His heart racing Elvis stuffed the com node back in his ear as his eyes flitted over the monitors. The one directed at the Urals showed a blistering mass of red, orange and blue clouds engulfing the entire thousand mile mountain range. He imagined the iron and minerals in those mountains turning to liquid. Peaks thousands of feet high were melting like molten lead.

How anyone would survive the inferno he didn't know, but his wife had to survive. She just had to.

"Sir?" said Maple from behind him.

"Yes, Maple what is it?"

"Sir, we have to go to the briefing. The signal alarm has been sounding for the last five minutes."

"Yes, of course." He decided to make a call before he left the com room. "L1 to L3."

"Go ahead, EP I've been monitoring the situation. What can I do?"

Good old, Pump, he thought, always watching my back. "Thanks, Pump. Keep watch over the Urals and let me know when the cloud clears and when you receive a signal. Okay?"

"No worries, 'ol buddy. You'll be the first to know when I hear the first peep."

"I'll call you later."

"Roger that. L3 out."

Elvis took out the node and put it back in the sterile holder he'd taken it from and stood. He glanced down at the monitor. The boiling terrible clouds rolled steadily east across the Russian steppes toward it's opposite number coming from the west. It appeared the two clouds of destruction would meet over Japan and together burn those islands off the map.

Elvis sighed then headed for the door to the corridor and the lift. The meeting better not take long. He wanted to get back here as soon as possible.

***

Elvis arrived back in the communications center alone. The briefing had lasted for two hours. He slumped down into the empty chair and leaned forward and rested his elbows on the consol. He closed his eyes. He wanted to cry but he was dry and numb from the pain of loss.

Sixty people on L1 had committed suicide after they witnessed the devastation. No one believed they'd kill themselves when the psychologists told them there would be suicides after impact. But he wasn't one of them. He agreed with the captain.

There was still hope that some of them would survive to carry on the human race.

While it was still early the news wasn't all bad.

None of the bunkers had yet made contact. And L2 hadn't checked in yet. But in addition to their station, L3, 4 and 5 were safe and the smaller asteroids following the planet killer hadn't yet been detected anywhere near the LaGrange orbits.

Tales From Space

Elvis made a mental note when he got through to the Urals he'd ask Ivan if he'd heard from Simone on L2. He needed to stay optimistic.

The gardens and farms on the stations and the water and air purification systems made the LaGrange stations completely self sufficient. They could survive and in twenty or thirty years they might even be able to join the survivors on the Earth to begin rebuilding civilization. At least that was the plan.

He wondered now if it was worth it for him. The chances Yvette survived the destruction in the Urals was slim. Even though it was unlikely he'd ever see her in person again any glimmer of hope that she lived was all he had to hold onto right now.

Just as he placed the com node in his ear the screen to his left blurred then steadied. It was the feed from L3 still focused on the Urals.

His heart seemed to skip a beat and he gasped when he saw the blink of bright red lights from beneath the clouds still obscuring the mountain range.

"L1 to L3. Come in, Pumper! Please come in!" He realized he was shouting but his excitement had bubbled over.

"Yeah, E I'm here. But don't scream at me, pal. What's up?"

"Did you see that?"

"What?"

Elvis edged forward in his chair and looked hard at the monitor. The light had disappeared there were only clouds now. "Uuh, I saw a light. A red flashing light."

"I don't see anything," said Pumper. "Let me run back the recording."

The cameras images were recorded in a protein based memory storage system containing 150 billion yottabytes of information. This memory capacity had been installed in each station so the collective knowledge of mankind would remain intact for ten million years.

"Yes, you're right. There it is. Interesting."

Elvis wanted to jump through the consol his impatience threatened to overwhelm him. "Well, what do you think?"

"Let me check. Give me a few seconds."

Silence. Elvis blinked away beads of sweat that trickled into his eyes and he fidgeted in his chair as if it had suddenly become uncomfortable. Since the chair automatically formed to the contours of the person sitting it this was impossible, but he could barely contain his nerves. Yvette could be alive somewhere down there and someone could be trying to signal them.

"Hummm, E my holo interface tells me this is a signal. A signal of human origin."

"What does it say?" Elvis blurted.

'Well, it's in Morse code..." Pumper's voice trailed off.

"Never mind all that. Is it from my wife?"

"Huh, no, E. It's an automated signal the computer was programmed to look for if the bunker..." Again his voice trailed off.

"You mean the message was to be sent if the bunker survived?"

"Huh, no. The opposite I'm afraid." Pumper paused. "I'm so sorry, E," he said his voice a whisper.

Elvis' shoulders slumped and a wave of grief washed over him in waves. She was dead. It was over. "Thanks, Pump."

He signed off and asked Maple to signal his shift replacement to take over for him. She did as he asked without question.

"I'll be in my cabin," he said before leaving the communications center.

Elvis arrived back in his cabin and sat down heavily on the bunk. He wondered what he'd do now. How would he carry on without the knowledge his beloved Yvette was alive and well? He shook his head and waited for the tears that would never come. He'd shed enough tears today.

He looked up and saw the monitor on the desk flash that a message was waiting for him. He didn't want to talk to anyone right now. All he needed was to be alone with his thoughts and his memories. It was all he had left.

He shrugged. There was no harm in checking the message. Whoever it was would have to wait for a reply but he could at least listen.

"Play message," he whispered.

The screen came to life and his eyes grew wide. It was Yvette.

Tales From Space

"Hi, E. It's me. I left this message for you a month ago when I was told the chances of survival were less than five percent." She paused and her watery, sky-blue eyes drifted to her right away from the camera then abruptly directly into the screen. It was as if she were looking right into his heart.

Elvis swallowed the bile that had risen to the back of his throat and let a breath slowly escape from between his dry lips. His hands trembled and a knot formed in his stomach. She looked so beautiful, so vulnerable.

"I love you, E. I always have and if there is another world beyond this one then I will wait for you as long as it takes. But I want you to do something for me. I want you to stay alive and help others to stay alive."

She paused again and her lips trembled. "And I want you to donate sperm to help the human race survive.

"I'm asking to do this because if you and other the men and women who survive don't do this then the human race's very existence will have been for nothing. I don't believe that and I know you don't believe it either.

"Please, Elvis, please promise me you'll do this. Please. And always remember, I love you."

The screen went dark.

He started when there was a knock on his door. He wiped the back of his hand across his eyes stood and walked to the door. He tapped the keypad next to the door.

The cabin door slid aside to reveal Maple standing in the corridor. Her brown eyes were slightly sad. He knew it wasn't real emotion but he appreciated the effort anyway.

"Yes, Maple what is it?"

"We just received word that L2 was damaged in a meteor shower, but they have managed to effect repairs and made contact a few minutes ago. No reported injuries."

Elvis nodded. "That is good news. Thanks, M."

The hologram nodded. "Yes, sir. I thought you'd like to know right away."

Elvis smiled at Maple then tapped the key pad next to the door and it closed.

Elvis walked to the desk where the monitor sat and sat on the chair facing the monitor. He stared at the screen.

Yes, he decided he'd do what Yvette wanted. She was right. He had a responsibility to humankind far greater than himself.

And he'd do it for Yvette.

Tales From Space

T.I.N. MEN

The U.S. Army issued ergonomic chair beneath Technical Sergeant Will Arnett trembled. Uncertain what was happening, Will's eyes drifted to the half empty glass of coke he'd earlier placed on the cup holder recessed into the consol next to his elbow.

Or was it half full? He'd always hated pop psychology, and was far too practical for such limited cerebral arguments. In his civilian life he had a PhD in software engineering and he programmed software. Everything in the world was either a one or a zero, nothing more.

He watched the sweet brown liquid splash up along the sides of the glass then his hazel eyes flitted sharply back to the three screens recessed into the consol in front of him. The deck shuddered again, only more violently this time. The screens provided him a 360 degree view of the dry, cactus and scrub brush dotted Arizona landscape surrounding the Styker reconnaissance vehicle.

He swallowed hard and his eyes went wide as an unbelievable site appeared on the center screen. He would later say he'd seen as a silver and gray robot that the onboard sensors said was over sixty feet in height suddenly appear out of the gloom of first light. It's body was human shaped with a wide chest and a head that swiveled as it scanned the desert. It moved in giant footsteps each the length of a Cadillac. It was headed westerly ninety degrees from his position.

It was barely past sunrise and the blue velvet sky glowed orange, yellow, and red as the sun's tendrils chased away the night. Since the desert can play tricks on you at sunrise Will blinked a few times, but the robot didn't vanish. This was impossible. *I must be dreaming.* If it were real though it would sure be fascinating.

Will had been on watch all night in the Styker on a military exercise in this patch of barren desert. As day approached he'd begun to wonder who he'd pissed off to rate this duty. Fortunately the Styker was a nuclear, biological, chemical reconnaissance vehicle, or NBCRV. This meant if they were properly equipped (which they were not) the five person crew could survive inside this tin can for up to two weeks.

Will's heart beat hard in his chest and he fought the urge to bolt from his chair as the massive robot on the screen took a step closer. The vehicle bounced on its undercarriage.

With trembling fingers, Will pulled down the mouth mike attached to his armored helmet he'd pushed out of his way. He needed to contact Lieutenant Sims in the command cab up front. The mike was voice activated, "Huh, sir."

No response.

"Sir! Lieutenant!"

The ground shook as the robot increased it's pace. It occurred to Will the Styker might not withstand being crushed underfoot by this mechanical monster. He didn't know why he thought this, but this robot's appearance had created an unusual situation after all.

"Yeah," came the sleepy reply of the Lieutenant who was sitting in the driver compartment forward of the surveillance control center. There was a hatch between the control center and the drivers compartment which the LT kept locked when he was up front with the driver.

The colonel had sent them out with himself, the lieutenant, and a rookie private named Pike as driver, on what he called a training mission. The mission objective was to simulate the loss of crew members to test how resourceful they could be with only three remaining crew versus a normal compliment.

Will swallowed hard when he recalled they didn't even have .50 cal ammunition for the M2 machine gun.

"What is it, grunt?" came the annoyed reply.

Will cringed. Sims was regular Army. He was reserves so Sims rode him pretty hard when ever the opportunity presented itself. "Sir, there's a giant robot coming straight at us. Sir." He added the second sir, because he knew how ludicrous what he'd just said sounded.

He watched the robot stop then the dark pupiless eyes set in the human shaped head swiveled and seemingly look right at him through the video screen. The remaining moisture in his mouth evaporated.

"A robot?" Sims grunted. "You bin watching cartoons back there?"

"Huh, no, sir. Believe me it's real. Turn on the external lights. Sir."

"OK, grunt, but if you've woken me for nothin' I'm gonna kick your ass all the way back ta base." Will heard the sound of a toggle switch through his head set.

"What the...." Sims voice trembled. "Pike! Wake up! Get us the hell outta here, we —"

Sims voice was cut off when every screen went dark and the familiar hum of the air exchange died. Will held his breath as he waited for the emergency generator to kick in, but nothing happened. They were dead in the water. Will sat in darkness. His breathing became shallow. The air already seemed stuffy and a few degrees warmer. A trickle of sweat ran down his left cheek and back.

Tales From Space

This is impossible. The M1135 NBC Reconnaissance Vehicle, or Styker, was designed to be impervious to Electro Magnetic Pulse attack. The exterior hull was constructed from a titanium alloy. Sloped armor would deflect an EMP attack. The interior walls were lined with a rubber liner to absorb electricity. The hull was also shielded from radiation by sealed lead paint, and the vehicle had its own internal air and recycling filtration system so a gas attack would be useless.

They were as safe as anyone on earth from non-conventional attack could be. Unfortunately, since the armor plating on the sides was thin, only 14 millimeters thick, conventional weapons, or a giant robot foot, could easily destroy them.

Will said a silent prayer. He was about to die.

Tales From Space

The vehicle around him trembled then he winced at he awful screech of metal on metal. He was gripped by a feeling of weightlessness. The vehicle around him shuddered as it was lifted into the air. His stomach muscles tighten as nausea enveloped him.

Will reached out to grip the edge of the consol and held on as tightly as he was able. Whatever was happening was causing his lean frame to alternate between straining against the restraining strap across his chest, he'd been insightful enough to have on, and become weightless as if her were floating in a swimming pool.

Fear welled from his belly as he realized the robot must have picked up the Styker and was carrying it as if it were a child's toy. But where were they going?

***

Tales From Space

After half an hour the swaying stopped and the vehicle bounced once more as it was placed on the ground. Will who's heart still pounded rapidly in his chest, and was frozen in his chair his sweaty fingers in a death grip on the chair arms. They'd stopped moving. Will let out a breath he'd been holding. He didn't much care where on terra firma he was, just that the shaking had stopped. He let out a breath he'd been holding and wiped his brow with the sleeve of his uniform jumper.

So far the robot hadn't threatened them.

"You in the M1135," said a booming mechanical voice over his headset. "Come out or we will destroy you."

Okay, that sounded like a threat. *But who was we?*

In the last thirty minutes, Will had mapped out a plan of action in his head. The robot was tall, it's hands were probably twenty feet or more from the ground. If he got out and took off running he would run between its legs before it could react. He'd find a hiding place the where robot was too large to follow until he could find a radio or a telephone to call the base. *What are my options?*

The Styker didn't have any surface-to-robot missiles, hand grenades, or as much as firecracker for that matter, so he couldn't fight the thing. Styker vehicles never carry weapons. And he couldn't surrender that would be cowardice in the face of the enemy, and if he survived the idea of spending time at Leavenworth prison cell made him the ultimate coward. The army *really* hated the word surrender. His superiors would not be amused.

No. All he could do was run for his life. To fight another day of course. It was a strategic retreat.

Tales From Space

Somehow he didn't think a giant robot that seized U.S. Army property was a friendly so it had to be fought. America was the land of shoot first ask questions later. That much was clear. But he didn't think of himself as the man for the job. *I'm a software engineer, not a warrior.*

The real questions were, how did a giant robot get into the middle of the Arizona desert, and why was it here?

He rose on unsteady legs from the chair and took in a deep breath to try and settle down his nerves. His cheeks puffed out as he released his breath stuttering gasps. He wiped the sweat from his brow with the back of his hand.

The emergency escape hatch was at the rear of the control center. He stumbled across the deck his hands reaching out in front of him. Quickly his finger tips made contact with the smooth walls of the vehicle. He managed to make his way to where he recalled the hatch was located without falling over one of the chairs at the workstations. He yelped as the toe of his right boot struck the hatch. He winced and swallowed hard.

Geez, that hurts.

The pain gradually subsided until finally he knelt down and felt for the hatch release. He found it and pulled the handle toward him. The hatch swung in and the control center was suddenly awash in blinding light. He closed his eyes tightly and waited for his eyes to adjust.

Holding one hand up to shield his eyes he blinked but managed to squeeze out the hatch without falling. *At least I can keep some of my dignity.*

So far his escape plan hadn't worked so well. He couldn't run blindly unable to see where he was headed could he?

"Stay right where you are, Sergeant." The voice was deep but mechanical.

Tales From Space

Knowing a threat when he heard one Will froze and waited. He suspected if it meant to kill him he would already be dead.

His eyesight gradually began to clear, sufficiently so he could make out fuzzy shapes. One he expected the other he did not.

The forbidding very tall, very wide shape had to be the robot. Beside the large blob of fuzz was a smaller more human sized shape. And it had curves. Female curves.

What the...? Where am I?

"You ok, sergeant?" said the woman.

Will blinked and the woman came into sharper focus. She was dressed in blue jeans, sneakers, and wore a bright orange tee shirt with the words MR. FUZZ emblazoned across her full breasts.

"Name's Arnett. Will Arnett. Technical Sergeant United States Army. Serial number —"

She laughed cutting him off in his name-rank-and-serial-number spiel. He had never been given an order to only provide these details, but he'd seen enough movies to know this was the procedure when captured by the enemy.

At least they seemed like an enemy. He eyed the shapely woman with her laughing blue eyes, dimple in her right cheek, and smirk on her lips. Funny thing was she wasn't acting like an enemy.

"Huh, sorry," he said. "That was about as stupid as I feel right now." Suddenly as if from nowhere anger welled up from the pit of his stomach.

She chuckled. He detected the scent of lemons coming from her direction. "I think it was kind of cute actually."

"I have a question for you," Will said.

She smiled and held up a tablet reader she'd been holding in her left hand. "Everything you need to know is on here. If you follow me we'll get some breakfast while you read."

Will frowned. She was avoiding the obvious and he was getting pissed off. "OK, I'll agree but you have to tell me your name first."

She chuckled and shook her head. "I'm sorry. We don't get many visitors so my social skills are somewhat lacking. My name's Holly Hope. I'm a scientist, like you."

***

The walked down the well lit corridor toward what appeared to be elevator doors at more than twenty feet away. *Where am I?*

"Are we underground?" he asked.

Holly nodded. "Oh, yes, about a mile down actually."

Will let go with a soft whistle. *Good thing I'm not claustrophobic.*

What was lightning the corridor wasn't obvious, but he suspected the ceiling was painted with a florescent paint backlit by low wattage light tubes. This told him they were trying to conserve power. Interesting. He wondered if they could generate enough power to fuel a sixty foot tall robot why they needed to conserve power. He mentally field the information away.

"So, Holly, where are my lieutenant, and the driver?" So far, Holly had been relaxed and wore an easy smile on her lips. She wasn't armed as far as he could tell, but she had made him curious, especially when she revealed she was had a PhD in biotechnology. And somehow she knew he was had a PhD in software engineering.

He frowned. *How does she know so much about me?* He looked at her walking beside him. She was sure cute, and apparently smart. He liked those qualities in a woman.

"Randall will drop them back on the spot in the desert where he picked you up," she said as casually as if she'd just made a run to the corner store for a candy bar. "No need to worry about them. They'll be fine."

He looked at her. "Who's Randall?"

She chuckled. *Is everything I say funny? I know I'm not funny.*

"Sorry. The robot who brought you here. His name's Randall." She used one index finger to make a twirling motion next to her head. "I can be so spiny sometimes. I forget you haven't been here before. Randall is one of our 'bots."

Will swallowed and his stomach tightened. "One?"

"Yeah. I mean, yes." They had reached the elevator doors. Affixed to the wall next to the doors was a black proximity reader. It had ridges in it's surface but was otherwise devoid of any markings.

Holly pulled a white plastic card about the size of a credit card from her right pocket and swiped it over the prox reader. The elevators doors parted. She stuffed the card back in her pocket then her eyes locked on his.

"You ready?"

Will swallowed hard. "For what?"

The sides of her mouth curled slightly but her eyes became flat. The humor had left her as if the air in a balloon was being released slowly. It unnerved him.

"To see the most incredible things you have ever seen."

Will wondered what she meant, but the scientist in him boiled to the surface. He had to know where that robot came from and where he was and who was behind this. Holly didn't have the specialty to build the robot. Once she told him about her specialty which was chemical engineering, he knew there had to have been others involved.

A knot of excitement shredded the fear had felt earlier. Like Mulder and Scully he had to know the truth.

"Yes, Holly, I am ready."

Her features changed back to the friendly grin and her eyes sparkled as they had before. "Great. You must meet, Dr. Good."

Will nodded.

They entered the elevator and the doors closed behind them. Holly used the card to swipe over another proximity card reader. There were no buttons and no floor numbers. The walls were bare except for the card reader.

There was a slight sensation of movement that was barely detectable. Will wondered if they were moving at all.

Holly became his tour guide. "We'll be traveling to the underground living quarters and research facilities twenty stories underground. The quarters house up to twenty-seven research scientists. We have several specialists who are experts in their fields; chemistry, biology, propulsion, exobiology, bioelectronics, biomechanics, and engineers in the fields of aerospace, and chemical engineering. We also have several PhD's who worked at JPL on interplanetary exploration."

"Is there a brochure?" Will muttered.

Holly looked at him with one eyebrow raised and laughed. "I like you already. You're funny."

The elevator stopped. The doors slid open. Will's jaw dropped. The vast expanse reminded him of his favorite '50's science fiction movie, Forbidden Planet.

The area was vast with diamond shaped corridors leading off a central common area teaming with people, some riding four wheeled electric trucks and some wearing white lab coasts carrying tablets and what looked like cell phones though he suspected they weren't cell phones. This far underground the most powerful cell on the commercial market wouldn't be able to get a signal.

The floors were polished black rock with veins of color running through it. And there were quite a number of robots. Not as big as the one that had snatched him, they were six feet tall and shiny silver in color. They had no eyes but must have sensors because they moved agley among the humans, who took no interest in them. It was as if robots were normal.

I'm clearly not in Kansas anymore. Or Arizona to be exact.

"I told you." Holly exited the elevator.

Will regained his composure and chased after her as she led him across the vast central hub. She was right. This was incredible. He caught up with her as she continued her tour guide spiel. She explained that the corridors led to the laboratories, the recreation area, a cafeteria and the living quarters. "We're going to the directors office first. Dr. Good is anxious to meet you."

Will noticed above each corridor was a large illuminated capital letter. They were about to enter corridor D. "Who is this, Dr. Good?"

"He's the director of the project. He has four PhD's, and has been director of the project since it started in 1967."

"Oh, really?" Will refrained from rolling his eyes. Good was an old man, probably with old man ideas. A robot walked past them in the corridor. *Well, maybe not that old.*

They passed several men and women who nodded to Holly as they went by but seemed to ignore him. They seemed a cold, unfriendly bunch. He wondered now why he was here.

Tales From Space

Finally they arrived outside a door recessed into the side of the corridor. There was no door handle or lock. Beside it was another prox card reader. Holly glanced at him and offered a closed mouth smile. She swiped her card over the reader and the door slid open and into the doorframe.

Beyond the entrance was a well lit office with a glass desk (he recognized it was made of plexi-glass not real glass. His old prof used to have one just like it). The desk had a flat screen in one corner and a pen set in a wooden holder near the front edge of the desk. The two items could not be more dissimilar. The old clashed with the new.

Two red leather chairs sat in front of the desk. Against one wall to his right was a matching red leather sofa. Hung on the wall over the sofa was a painting of the Saturn V rocket in flight.

They entered the office together with Holly slightly ahead as the lead.

Sitting behind the desk sipping a dark liquid from glass was a small man. He looked about the size of a ten year old, only the steel gray hair that ringed his bald spot, and the wrinkles around the intense green eyes told Will he was much older than he at first appeared.

"Sit down, Sergeant," the man said, his tone gentle but firm. Will sat down burying his hands in his lap to hide the trembling. "I'm sorry about the dramatic manner of your arrival, but it couldn't be helped." Maybe this was a bad idea after all.

"I'm Dr. Oz Good. You can call me, Dr. Good." He set the glass on the desk. His eyes narrowed and his smooth brow creased as he frowned. "Never call me the Wizard of Oz."

Holly struggled in vain to stifle a snort. When she did let go, Dr. Good's eyes shot to her and he scowled. "Leave us, Dr. Hope." His tone was tight and disapproving.

Will looked at Holly. Her cheeks were flushed red and her eyes avoided the directors glare. She nodded her head slightly then said, "Yes, sir. I've got to check my most recent test results anyway." Holly turned left the office the doors sliding closed behind her.

Dr. Good's features relaxed and he steepled his fingers and seemed to studying him. Will was startled and jumped in the chair when Dr. Good suddenly burst out laughing. He squirmed until Dr. Good stopped and wiped the tears from his eyes with his long thin fingers. "So, Sergeant. I'm told you have a PhD in software engineering?"

Will cleared his throat. He prayed he wouldn't sound like a frog. "Uhhh, yes sir, Dr. Good...sir." *I sound like the biggest idiot on the planet.*

"Good. Great in fact. We need a person with your qualifications." He paused and the smile dissipated as his expression shifted to somber. "The last software engineer was...lost." He nodded and stood up behind the desk. Will detected the hesitation in his Dr. Good's voice.

Something bad must have happened, but what? "So you want me to work for you?"

Good smiled and walked around the desk and moved to sit on the sofa. He waved to Will to join him. Will sat down. "Yes, but it's up to you. Of course I will have to explain what this is all about and about our mission."

Will nodded. "Of course." This all sounds a bit cryptic. He needed answers. "Where are we?" he asked.

"I assume you've heard of Area 51?" Will nodded again and licked his lips. Aliens. These guys are nuts. "We are Area 52. Our facility, our mission, our funding, our existence is above top secret. The only people who know about us are at the top of the U.S. government. The President, the Secretary of Defense, and the Chairman of the Joint Chiefs." His eyes narrowed and his lips formed a thin line. "No one else." He rose to his feet and began to pace the tiled floor. "Other than those who work here of course. No one knows about us, or must know about us."

Will's heart beat faster at that last part. If he told anyone about this place and the robots, he had a feeling it wouldn't be good for his health. "Ummm, Dr. Hope said something about a project?"

Dr. Good stopped pacing and turned to face him. "Our project is called TIN Men."

"By the name I'm guessing you build robots?"

Good arched one eyebrow. "That's only half the story actually."

Will arched an eyebrow. "What's the other half?"

"We're in a robot race that's been going on since 1967."

Will's curiosity threatened to bubble over. "Robot race? Like a marathon?"

Dr. Good laughed and crossed his arms over his narrow chest. "No. Not that kind of race. A cold war style race." Good dropped into silence.

Will stared back at Dr. Good uncertain what or who he was talking about. Russia wasn't the USSR, in fact the country was a shell of it's former self. China was an economic power. Sure, they had a large military, but funding an ultra secret robot program seemed a little beyond their means. Iraq? Iran? No. No way. The Saudi's, the North Koreans? The European Union? Unlikely. "A cold war? With whom?"

"Who do you think?"

Will shrugged. "I don't know...Japan?"

Dr. Good's eyebrows rose in obvious surprise. "How did you know that?"

"I guessed."

Dr. Good moved across to this desk and picked up his glass of coke. He took a swig and offered Will a glass, which he accepted. After he filled a glass from the bottle in the bar fridge behind his desk he sat once again in the red leather executive chair.

He explained. "As you know Japan has become a technologically advanced society. Many Japanese have a love for science fiction, and robots, giant monsters. They started a giant robot program, so in order for the United States to keep it's technological edge we began ours at the same time."

Will snorted. "You do realize how stupid that sounds, right?"

"Yes, I know. But we have been in a race with the Japanese ever since. There are unconfirmed rumors that India and China have begun early work on their own robot programs, but our latest intelligence reports say they're years away from a practical working prototype."

Will stood he'd had enough. "You know this all sounds crazy. We're talking about robots!" He moved to the desk and stood staring at Dr. Good. "It's science fiction. It's not real."

Dr. Good eased back in his chair causing the leather to squeak. He arched an eyebrow. "You met, Randall, and saw the worker drones in the corridors did you not?"

Will grimaced. He was right of course. As unbelievable as it sounded the robots were real. But was everything else he said also true? "OK, Dr. Good, I'll concede that point, but I find it hard to believe a robot cold war has been going on for over forty years, and no one knows about it."

"We have developed a drug that wipes selected memories of anyone who comes into contact with our facility or research."

Will sensed Good was hiding something from him, though hiding wasn't the correct term. A better term would be evasion. He wasn't answering his questions directly. For the first time in a long time, Will knew he was being tested. And this made him mad. He'd hated tests since Mrs. Chopnik sprang that surprise arithmetic test on his first grade class.

"Listen, Dr. Good, let's stop beating around the mechanical bush and you tell me what's going on and why I'm here."

Dr. Good surprised him when his narrow features broke into a wide smile. Had he said something funny? Or had he just sounded so stupid all a person could do was laugh at him.

Tales From Space

"Dr. Arnett, welcome aboard." He stood behind his desk and held out his right hand.

Will took Dr. Good's hand in his. His skin was warm and the grip was firm. But what had he just joined? Will released his grip and sat down again. "Dr. Good, please tell me something important. I've come aboard *what* exactly?" He blurted out the last word. His frustration meter had gone through the roof.

Dr. Good's expression became very serious. "I'm offering you a chance to join Project TIN Men as the lead software development engineer. It is quite an honor, believe me. You'll lead a team of ten of the best software engineers in the world, and you'll be paid more than Google or Microsoft or Facebook would ever pay you. I can say with no exaggeration in one year you'll make enough to buy your own private island. And you'll have enough money to buy a lifetime supply of those chocolate mint patties you love so much. Honestly? You could buy the company that makes those confections."

Will took a sip of the coke and then dragged in a deep breath. The soda tickled his taste buds and its sweetness lingered in tongue even after he swallowed. He released the breath, "What's the catch?"

Dr. Good's lips formed a tight smile. "Good. Direct. I like that." He paused and looked away. With his back now to Will he said, "We will transplant your brain into the body of a robot much like Randall so you won't require air or water. Not where you're going. Then you'll travel to the moon where you'll help to build a base on the dark side of the moon."

Will's heart raced. Moon base? His brain?

***

Two months later, Will lay on an operating table waiting for the electrodes to be affixed to the four input terminals surgically implanted in his skull. The terminals were inserted into his frontal lobe, parietal lobe, occipital lobe, and temporal lobe. His brain wouldn't actually be removed and placed in the robots control center, but somehow the scientific team had found a way to transfer every experience, every memory, every instruction accumulated in his lifetime to the robots artificial brain.

His body would be stored in stasis while he went to the moon. The dark side of the moon to be exact. The team would be composed of seventeen robots and the base would take six months to complete.

He was pleased, Holly would be accompanying, her transferred brain also encased in a robot body.

He'd been fully briefed on the mission. They were to build a base on the dark side of the moon hidden from Earthly eyes. The reason he'd been given was the base was being built by an international organization funded by the G25. The funding was secret and the project was secret. The organization was code named The International Network or T.I.N.. The code name for the bot's was TIN Men.

    He was not only chosen for his expertise in his field, but because his parents died in a car accident two years ago, he was an only child, and had no other family. He'd begun to enjoy being a part of something. In the army he had felt more like an outsider, the regular grunts detested soldiers who were smarter than they were.

    To be honest most gerbils were smarter than most of the men and women he served with in the recon unit he'd been assigned to.

    While for the most part the story rang true, Will, still thought there were gaps in the tale that bothered him. Holly had admitted her reservations as well after they'd slept together.

She had been working at MIT when she was approached as asked to join the project. She'd agreed when she was advised Dr. Good was the project director.

An interesting factoid about her was she was also an orphan like himself. In fact everyone he'd encounter involved with the project had no family. He couldn't shake the uncomfortable thought this meant they wouldn't be missed if something went wrong.

But what could go wrong? Their brains were transferred to living machines, then they'd slip through an energy field that transmitted matter thousands of miles in the blink of an eye.

A matter transmitter terminal was already on the moon near the site where the base would be constructed. The European-China Space Agency had sent a robot space craft with the terminal aboard to the moon and by all reports it landed safely. Some worker droids were to set up the terminal. Recent orbital surveys confirmed the droids had completed the set up. But the real question was had the droids put it together properly.

The worker droids could have built the moon base as well, but it would have taken them decades due to their limited ability to adjust to unexpected situations. They were only capable of being programmed to respond to pre-determined situations. And not every situation could be covered by the programmers

Dr Good had been evasive about why they needed to work so fast and take such risks, but Will suspected there was much more going on than he knew.

Also, any breakdowns wouldn't be fixed, the resources hadn't been supplied to fix any mechanical problems if the droids broke down. Yet.

But this was all about to change. The plan was for the TIN men to build a repair facility as the first phase of the project.

"All TIN men to the departure bay!" said a deep male voice over the facility wide public address system.

Will set the giant robot in motion and walked the massive tunnels headed for the departure bay. Holly's lime green and soft gray two tone bot joined him. He was pleased to see her.

"Hi, Holly, you ready?"

Her bot swiveled it's head to face his and nodded. "For sure. But I wish they'd refer to us females as TIN women."

We'd been having this discussion for months but it was a spurious argument because the robots were sexless. The human sexual urges and feelings of the brain implanted in the artificial brain wasn't relevant. Especially as we communicated by telepathic means and were about to enter an inhospitable environment. In such a place sex where wasn't relevant, and these bodies weren't built with the right bits and pieces anyway.

"Next time, Ok?" Will joked.

Holly chuckled. "Yeah, okay."

We soon arrived in the departure bay where the transport technician had set up the first test of the matter transmitter. There were going to be five tests before they were sent through.

First they would send a Camera and Recording Bot, or CRB, to monitor the reception terminal. The CRB central processor and sealed camera was built on a platform set on rubber composite tracks. Immediately upon arrival on the moon it would move off the platform then send pictures back of the remaining tests. Of course if no signals came back this would mean the droids had failed to set up the receiving transport receiver properly.

    Will watched the technicians guide the robot onto the large round platform that rose above the shiny tile floor of the bay. Near the outer walls were five consol's where technicians sat monitoring everything from energy levels of the matter transporters systems, to humidity, and the telemetry data provided by a satellite net transmitted from high earth orbit to a network of satellites orbiting the moon. This would be their lifeline until the job was complete for Will and Holly and the rest of the team. There were going to be six of us building the station.

    Will and Holly watched as the technicians called out data they received from their consol's as a humming sound began to grow in intensity. Finally the humming reached its zenith and there was a brilliant flash of light that seemed to consume the CRB. When the light dissipated the bot was gone.

"Sir!" It was one of the telemetry technicians calling to Dr. Good who stood across the room at another consol watching the power level indicators. He was really proud of the fact they had finally harnessed the power of a nuclear reactor that generated more power than the Hiroshima bomb. He'd been working on it since the project began in 1967.

Dr. Good looked up. "Yes? What is it, Jamal?"

"Sir. There is no signal from the CRB."

Dr. Good's brow wrinkled and Will recognized the confusion on his narrow features. "Give it a few minutes."

Suddenly the technician yelled out. His face paled and he waved one hand wildly at the screen in his consol. "Sir. You better come look at this."

Tales From Space

Dr. Good nodded and stuffed his hands in the pockets of his ankle length white lab coat. He walked casually across the room seemingly unconcerned over the urgency in Jamal's tone. Will noted his brow was knitted and he was humming, both signs he was in reality worried. Will sensed something bad had happened.

Will moved his robot body closer to the consol and at an angle he could see the screen. what he saw made him, for the first time, reconsider his reasons for agreeing to be part of this project.

On the screen he could see a wide view of a field of gray rock and sand under an ink black sky dotted with points of unblinking light. There were also blackened shards of metal scattered like leaves across the moon's surface. From the angle of the image Will suspected the camera was on its side.

It was clearly evidence of an explosion. Now Will was worried. The only thing that could explode was the nuclear power source for the transmitter reception terminal, and the internal power source for the droids. The good thing was the camera aboard the CBR had survived the explosion which meant the mostly likely source of the explosion was a droid.

The root of this problem was how this had happened. Was it coincidental the arrival of the CBR occurred at the exact moment of a droid exploding. And was the transporter terminal damaged by the explosion.

Dr. Good crossed his arms and studied the screen his features scrunched in a scowl. "I wasn't expecting this so soon."

"Dr. Good," piped up Holly's bot. She had approached the consol from the opposite side from where Will was standing. "*What* were you expecting?"

Will thought her tone was harsh, but he too was surprised Dr. Good had withheld information from them. "Yes, doc, Holly and I want what's going on."

Dr. Good sighed and his shoulders sagged. He took off his wire rimmed glasses and massaged the bridge of his nose with his thumb and forefinger as if he had a headache, his eyes were closed. Suddenly he stopped and grunted as he put his glasses back on.

He reached for the com system button on the consol and punched the red button which changed to green meaning the public address system had been activated.

"Attention all TIN Men Project personnel, this is Dr. Good." He paused and took in a deep breath then continued. "I've been asked a rather important question and while I'm forbidden to reveal certain facts recent events on the moon lead me to believe you must all know why we must build the base on the moon and maintain absolute secrecy.

"I'm certain you have all been wondering about the rumored hidden agenda. I appreciate you have all followed orders without question while bringing this project to fruition. If we fail in our endeavors we, meaning all of humanity, will be faced with a future too terrible to imagine at the hands of a megalomaniac bent on total world domination.

Dr. Good glanced at Will's bot then his eyes drifted to Holly's. "Our TIN Men will be the front line in this war. A war against a secret organization calling itself The Mayday Directorate. The leader of The Mayday Directorate is a brilliant scientist named Dr. Bartholomew Good, my brother."

***

Will heaved the large gray and black rock across the moonscape. In the one sixth Earth gravity it flew more than a thousand yards before landing in a cloud of moon dust. They would have the area where they'd sink in the foundation posts for the new base cleared in a couple of hours. Will and the rest of the TIN Men had only been here for ten hours and already the base construction was well underway.

Holly was with a team of the surviving droids extracting ice from the shaded sides of craters. They would place the ice in the evaporation tank two of their colleagues were busily constructing. Once the tank was powered up the ice would melt and provide fresh water for the base's eventual inhabitants.

They'd waited for three months until a force of armed TIN Men could be built to provide security for the base construction. Will wasn't happy to see an armed presence but The Mayday Directorate had been prevented from doing any further sabotage.

Tales From Space

It was discovered that their agents had planted bombs inside some of the worker droids. Though a couple exploded when the CBR went through the matter transporter they hadn't damaged the device so severely as to stop the transport of a repair crew of droids.

After the repairs Will, Holly and the rest of the team had been sent to the moon and work had begun.

Dr. Good explained that his brother and he had started the project at Area 52 together, but his brother and he had a falling out. He hadn't heard of his brother until The Directorate destroyed the Columbia space shuttle.

Once the moon base was completed it would begin it's real work. It would be the jumping off point to send deep space missions throughout the solar system to find minerals and water and other building blocks for the eventual exploration of planets where the first signs of extraterrestrial life had been discovered.

Will was excited about the future and hoped his TIN man would survive for many years to come so he could be part of the next great adventure. Humankind was going to finally make it's mark in the galaxy.

Will stopped working when the ground began to shake. He hoped it was a meteor strike but then the early warning meteor detection grid would have alerted them of an impending strike. He had a sinking feeling he knew what caused the disturbance of the moon's crust.

Suddenly the horizon lit up with gold and red flashes. There was no denying it they were being attacked. And the TMD bots had used cloaking technology in the past but every time it had been scouts and they were quickly destroyed by the TIN Men security team. Somehow this felt different.

Tales From Space

Will had to brace the bot's legs to keep from falling over when the ground heaved beneath him and a cloud of dust shot into the star studded sky to the west of his position. The gray dust quickly blocked out the stars. Will knew the weapon ports Dr. Good had installed in his robot were about to become useful. He had hoped to avoid the coming conflict. The directorate didn't want to talk, they wanted to destroy. Now it was war.

The TMD was planning to stop them before they could complete the moon base. Holly told him they were paid by a coalition of pirate states led by the Texas Syndicate and the Welsh Dominion. They were paying TMD to destroy the TIN Men project. They planned to take over the interstellar exploration of deep space, not for peaceful purposes, but for conquest and monopolizing resources.

They had to be stopped, and the TIN Men had to do it.

"Sentry Seven reporting a breach in the defensive line. There are three —" The com went silent. Sentry Seven had been taken out."

It was time for action. Will sent a message through the com net. "Dr. Arnett to TIN Men and all sentries. Initiate plan alpha-two-nine."

Will counted acknowledgements and realized fourteen sentries had been lost already. Will walked to the edge of worksite and stopped. Clouds of moon dust had risen to blot out the star field across the horizon.

He'd deploy the laser gun in the left arm of the robot then the rail gun with the armor piercing projectiles in the right arm. He also engaged the energy shield that he hoped would hold off the TMD bot's weapons long enough so he could launch a counter attack. Unfortunately the weapons had been deployed so quickly the testing of the shields had been inconclusive. Will wanted to shudder at the memory of the chest plate of the test bot melting and fusing the torso.

The plan was to deploy the TIN Men and the surviving sentries in an oval shape and guard the base by repelling any attacks. The sentries were smaller therefore they'd be in front of the TIN Men who were taller and better armed. It was a classic order of battle design used by the British (though they used squares not ovals), and the Roman legions before them.

Soon Will counted thirty five sentries and looking around he saw his six companion TIN Men, including Holly who was directly behind him facing outward, her back to him. He worried she would get hit, but Dr. Good's armor should protect her. He hoped.

Then sentries quickly deployed per the plan and there was an uneasy lull. Silence no com traffic as they waited for the enemy. If Will's

TIN Man could smell it would smell the sweat, the oil and grease and the heat of the laser warming to firing temperature. But since the suits didn't allow for such sensory data he would just imagine it.

Suddenly from over the horizon six large TMD robots appeared. Their armored bodies were black and silver and from the look of them they appeared to have missile launchers affixed to their left shoulders and rail guns attached to their right arms. This wasn't going to be an easy fight. The other Dr. Good had obviously anticipated the TIN Men's weapons and tactics.

This was further supported by their spreading out so as not to create one massive target. They'd be in range in ten seconds.

Time seemed to pass slower as Will silently counted down the seconds. His targeting scanner beeped and he pressed the firing button for the rail gun. The first hardened steel/titanium projectile shot off the rail and tracked to the target, one of the enemy bots to his right. The projectile struck enemy bot in the center of it's chest plate and it shot backward off it's feet. It landed in a cloud of moon dust broken in half at the waist. the legs wouldn't work without the torso.

Will was pleased. One shot, one bot out of action. This wasn't going to be such a difficult battle after all.

A flash of a laser beam shot across the no mans land from one of the enemy bots. It struck Dr. Helen Taskers TIN Man and sliced her torso in two. It was almost as if her shields weren't on.

"Will." It was Holly. "I've picked up a low frequency wave that's interfering with our shield generators." She paused and the information sunk in. If the enemy was able to do this then maybe all of their systems could be compromised.

"Helen!" Will called.

"Yes," Helen said her voice trembling with fear.

"Check your generator power level."

There was a short pause then she replied, "It's reading zero. And it's not related to the damage I've sustained."

Now Will was worried. The enemy had the upper hand, but the question was how had they learned to defeat their shields so easily? They still had the EMP weapon if the battle became hopeless. The electro magnetic pulse would take out the enemy, but would also immobilize the TIN Men. And it might wipe the neural connectors. Theoretically the EMP might result in brain death for the TIN Men as well as the enemy so it had to be a weapon of last resort. His orders from Dr. Good were simple: do not lose. He was in charge. He was determined to win this battle at all costs. The future was at stake.

A soft beep told him the enemy robots were now in range. He issued an order. "All TIN Men fire at will."

Will and the other TIN Men launched everything they had at the approaching enemy force. Their missiles and lasers struck the enemy bots and knocked them backward. The five remaining enemy robots were down. It had been easy — too easy."

"Cease fire," Will ordered.

When the first enemy robot suddenly stood up, Will's arterial heart rate increased. It looked unharmed from the missile impact.

Oh, oh, no champagne and caviar for us tonight. Celebrations for an easy victory would have to wait. They could shoot them again ,but Will suspected this would be as ineffective as the first time.

"All TIN Men, stand your ground and be ready to deploy close quarter weapons." The acknowledgements came back as Will changed his laser to a ten foot long titanium sword shaped blade. The others too had their bladed weapons at the ready.

The enemy robots had started moving again only this time they were covering more ground. They were quickly taking long sustained strides. Will knew the other TIN Men would keep fighting until the end.

Another laser sliced Allisters robot in half at the waist. Will's mood darkened. He suspected now they had a plan. They were immobilizing the TIN Men but not destroy the fused human AI brain. They would transplant the fused brain into a new robot body they could control. It was the worst possible scenario. The loss of free will.

"Allister?"

"I'll be okay, Will. A little crazy glue and I'll be right as rain."

Will smiled inside. Allister was such a joker. "No, worries, old buddy. We'll get you fixed up as soon as we have these bastards taken care of."

"Thanks, Will."

Suddenly the enemy attacked.

Will fouhgt back clashing with the nearest enemy bot. He quickly separated an arm from the upper torso of an enemy bot with a single swipe of his blade. It was then he noticed one of the enemy bots hanging back from the others. He watched with horror as it pressed a button on a panel on it's right arm and suddenly he lost control of his body. Now he was a brain trapped in a nonfunctioning robot body. He was unable to move. *I have to move. I can't let them win.*

He stole a glance at Holly and saw she had retracted her blade and moved her robot to stand beside the enemy bot that had taken them all out of action. Will sent a command to the EMP weapon he'd secreted in one of the sentry bots. *No, not Holly*! Will wanted to cry.

His body jerked as if struck by lightning and the world around him disappeared.

***

When Will's systems came back on line he found himself laying on his back on the moon's surface staring up at the star strewn milky way galaxy. He tested his robot's limbs and found everything worked.

Getting to his feet he looked around and saw the remaining TIN Men were also getting to their feet. All expect, Holly who lay still on her back next to the leader of the TMD attack force.

He knew without asking their systems were fried and their AI brains along with all their memories were wiped clean.

Dr. Good had been correct. There was a traitor in their ranks, who had not only sabotaged the worker bots in an attempt to destroy the CBR thus jeopardizing the mission. And this same traitor that provided the frequency of their shields to the enemy. Dr. Good hadn't thought they'd be able to do this unless they had help from an insider with the highest security level. Will didn't think anyone on the team could be a traitor. Especially not Holly. He'd been wrong.

Holly. Will didn't know why she did it, but one day he'd find out. When Holly's brain died her body stored in stasis back on Earth became an empty shell. She was gone forever.

Will was determined to ensure one day the other Dr. Good would pay for her death and the destruction he'd caused.

Only Dr. Good and he knew they're robot bodies had been hardened against EMP attack.

The trap had worked perfectly. It had brought the traitor out into the open. Too bad it turned out to be Holly.

"Will?" It was Allister.

"Don't worry, Allister, and you too, Helen. We'll get you both fixed up. I can't have you slacking off. We have a lot of work to do still."

Helen spoke next. "Sorry, about Holly, Will."

"It's no ones fault but hers," Will said and he meant it.

The TIN Men would survive and they would compete their task. Former Technical Sergeant Will Arnett was determined to make it happen.

Tales From Space

The Secret

He hadn't slept much in the past few days and he dreaded what the doctor would say when he saw him. A com whistle sounded interrupting his thoughts.

"Yes, sir?" Com officer Bell's gentle voice was at its best professional tone today. Allen smiled to himself. Alicia Bell was the best in the fleet, but he wasn't going to tell her that.

"Get me Admiral Smyth," said Allen. Smyth was in charge of ship assignments at Fleet HQ.

"Yes, sir I...."

Allen interrupted his communications officer. "Belay that Lieutenant...and Bell?"

"Yes, sir?"

"Thank you." Allen hit the com button again cutting off any further comment by his loyal communications officer.

Allen often relished the fact that his crew was so often behind him in difficult situations. This time however they were asking too much of him, and in some ways he agreed with them. This time it was personal so he wanted to leave his crew out of it. Though he knew they wouldn't let this decision rest without a fight.

A hail from the control panel next to the door to his quarters interrupted his commiserations.

"Open," he said, his voice hollow in his ears. He knew who it was and he didn't need, or crave, advice.

The doors slid open with a *whoosh* and Dr. Sanji Kupta, his medical officer, waltzed in holding a bottle of what could only be brandy in his left hand. His haggard features were grim and the usual glint in his brilliant brown eyes was absent.

"Hanson," said Kupta, with a slight nod of his head as he sat in one of the empty chairs next to the desk.

Allen eyed Doc Kupta who sat in silence, the amber bottle with its curved neck sitting unopened next to him on the desks cool, dull gray surface. For his part Kupta seemed to be studying Allen as if he were one of his lab specimens.

"You know, Doc, I've never felt this way when a crew member is transferred. I mean for God's sake this isn't normal for a man in my position. They're demanding far too much of me this time."

Kupta crossed his thin arms across his narrow chest while a single dark, gray-streaked, eyebrow frowned at his captain.

"That's what worries me, Hanson."

Allen rose from his chair and began to pace the length of the cabin his booted footsteps dulled by the thick pile of the blue and gray carpet. His arms waved about as he spoke as if to accentuate his words.

Kupta watched in silence as his friend vented his anger and frustration.

Command had picked a fine time to eliminate the Captain's Yeoman program from the fleet's crew manifests.

Kelly Amstead, his yeoman of more than a year, was a close friend to many of the crew onboard, especially Bell, and extremely popular with everyone.

Consequently, the crew fully expected Allen, as captain of the *Earth's Daughter,* one of only fifteen such vessels in the fleet, to easily persuade command to have Amstead reassigned here, where she belonged.

Tales From Space

After all Captain Hanson Allen had battled alien's aggressors, and survived strange spatial phenomena of all descriptions with distinction and valor and triumphed every time.

Surely a few stuffed shirts at command would be easily swept aside by their young, head-strong captain. The rumor mill predicted Kelly would be back aboard within the week.

Deep down the doc suspected Allen had a more singular than altruistic reasons in mind than a simple question of leadership.

Naturally, Hanson Allen being Hanson Allen he'd made every effort to shield his personal feelings from all those around him. Kupta knew Hanson's true feelings for Kelly Amstead were buried somewhere deep inside him.

Hanson had always prided himself in his ability to keep his personal feelings concerning any one member of the crew from affecting his decisions. Fleet captains were expected to put the safety of the ship and its crew ahead of personal considerations. Kupta knew Hanson believed in this principal, but he also knew the man hated it.

There had been many times even he and second officer Miller, as Hanson's best friends, were on the outside when it came to the captain's personal entanglements, and there had been many.

"Amstead has done so much to keep morale amongst this crew the highest in the fleet. Her work with those women on Synar II, and on other countless occasions is a credit to the service. She's the epitome of what the Federation stands for. Now they want her back at command? As what? Some admiral's desk jockey? Mark my words, Doc, I'm going to get to the bottom of this even if it means my command."

Doc snorted and shook his head. "You know you don't mean that, Hanson." He reached over and uncorked the bottle of brandy then reached into the hidden drawer where Hanson kept his glasses.

After retrieving two of the short clear glasses he poured two generous measures of the potent drink. The odor of sweet brandy filled the room. "Com'on have a drink with your doctor."

Hanson cast a disapproving glance at his long time friend then shrugged his broad shoulders and moved to the desk. He pulled out a second chair and sat down to face Kupta, a look of annoyance in his blue eyes.

"I don't need any lectures, Doc."

Kupta gave Allen a lopsided grin as he held up both hands in surrender. "No argument here. This is social call. After all I'm a doctor not a bartender. You need advice you go back to that little bar on Argelius III."

Allen let slip a small smile at Kupta's mention of the pleasure planet they'd visited years before. His expression softened.

He picked up the glass of brandy and downed the contents in one swallow. His face registered the heat of the alcohol as the burning liquid slid down his throat. "Of course you're right, doctor." He sighed heavily then with the thumb and index finger of his right hand he rubbed his eyes.

Kupta watched with more than a passing interest. He took a generous sip of his brandy then said, "You've got to get some sleep before you drop. You're no good to anyone if you fall asleep at the helm."

Now Allen chuckled, his mood shifting. "I thought that's why I paid a certain navigator named Milton."

Kupta joined Allen in quiet laughter as he poured Hanson another glass of brandy then topped up his own half empty glass.

The atmosphere in the room was brighter than it had been only moments before.

"What do you plan to do, captain?" Kupta said his face reverting to a grim expression.

Allen gazed hard into Kupta's eyes and said, "I'm going to pressure Milo Smyth to reassign her back to the *Earth's Daughter*."

"And how in heavens name do you propose to do that? I mean you can't go threatening to blow holes in him, or try that poker-bluff maneuver again. Milo Smyth's no fool and he out ranks you."

Allen nodded and took a tentative sip of the fragrant brandy "Milo and I go back to the academy together." Allen shrugged. "I'm going to appeal to his sense of fair play. If there's one thing I know about Milo he's a fair man, and he knows that a star ship runs as much on its leadership as it does on its stomach."

Kupta frowned. "So you're expecting this desk jockey to understand that your crew is about to lynch you if you don't by some miracle get him to reassign Kelly Amstead?"

Allen smiled weakly and nodded. Kupta was about to add something when they were interrupted by another communication whistle. It was Bell's voice that came over the speaker next Allen's private viewer. "Bridge to Captain Allen."

Allen glanced at Kupta and cast the doctor a thin smile, as if to say they'd been saved by the bell from a knock down drag out argument.

"Do you want me to leave?" asked Kupta.

Allen shook his head and hit the white com button next to the speaker with his thumb. "Allen here."

"Captain, I have Admiral Smyth on viewer for you, sir."

"Put him through to my viewer, Lieutenant."

"Aye, sir." One of Allen's eyebrows went up his forehead, his eyes remained fixed on the doctors. The disappointment that the communication would be private was very evident in Bell's voice.

Allen hit the com button again to cut off his communication officer as the viewer on his desk shimmered and the image of Admiral Milo Smyth appeared.

Smyth's gentle brown eyes smiled warmly when he saw Allen. "Hanson. I received your message. You communications officer said it was urgent. Something about a planet-wide disaster?"

Allen glanced at Kupta and winced. He'd have to have a long talk with a certain lieutenant about message priorities.

Allen looked back at Smyth his expression changing to a sheepish grin. "Sorry, Milo, I think my crew may be getting a little space happy."

Smyth chuckled. "No problem, Hanson, I'm certain you'll ensure it never happens again."

Allen cringed inside. *A fine way to start with me about to make demands.*

Allen sighed. "Yes, sir. " Allen paused to gather his thoughts and his expression became hard. "The real reason I called is to discuss the transfer of one of my staff."

Milo looked surprised. "Oh?"

"Yeoman Kelly Amstead was transferred two days ago and is headed back to Earth. I agree with elimination of the captain's Yeoman program but—"

"Hold on, Hanson," said Smyth. "I would have expected your first officer to have briefed you by now."

Now it was Allen's turn to look surprised. Kupta frowned and the expression on his face said he was boiling inside, but he managed to remain silent even though it was obviously a struggle.

"Miller hasn't said anything…"

"As you know Hanson all crew assignments are done…"

"Through the first officer…yes, I know, Milo. Do you happen to know why she was transferred?"

"You should discuss that with your first officer. Smyth out." The viewer went dark.

Kupta burst out before Allen could say anything. "Why didn't he tell you? Damn it, he knows the crew's upset. That scheming bastard ahs always been after the top job. He's trying to make you look bad. I otta …"

"Enough, Doc." Allen cut off the doctor with a warning glance then hit the com button again. "Allen to Miller."

Allen knew Miller was seated in the captain's chair on the bridge so he answered the hail immediately. "Miller here, sir."

"Report to my quarters immediately."

"Aye, sir, I am on my way." As usual the first officer's voice contained its standard issue calm.

With a few minutes the door to Allen's quarters opened and the blue shirted figure of Commander Bart Miller came in, his hands clasped behind his back. His coal black eyes and steely gaze met Allen's as he moved to stand beside the desk.

"Why don't you join us, Miller?" said Kupta raising his half filled glass of brandy in a toast, his gravely voice heavy with sarcasm.

"As you well know, doctor, I do not imbibe alcohol." Miller wasn't his real name. He was born on Regilus One and joined the fleet as a exobiologist sixteen years ago.

Since his race is known for a naturally calm manner he was nominated for command school at the academy, and had climbed the ranks ever since.

He'd been second in command of the *Earth's Daughter* for five years. Allen had been captain for three of those years

"Knock it off you two," said Allen. "Sit down." Allen nodded to the other empty chair across the desk from the doctor.

Miller did as directed and sat down with his hands folded in his lap.

"Explain," said Allen his voice even.

"Sir?" said Miller.

"You know what he means, Miller," said Kupta.

A lone dark eyebrow over Miller's right eye rose up his pale forehead. "If you are referring to Kelly Amstead then I am unable to explain."

Allen couldn't believe his ears. It was as if his first officer had been expecting this line of inquiry. "That's an order, Mr. Miller." For the first time since he'd assumed command of the *Earth's Daughter* from Norm Kilani he was second guessing himself about his decision to keep Miller as his first officer.

At the time Norm told him Miller was the finest second in command in the fleet. With this latest turn of events Allen now had his doubts.

"I am unable to follow that order. Sir."

Allen snorted in frustration his eyes narrowing. "Well then at least tell me why."

"I am unable…"

"For pity's sake, Miller, you have to tell us something!" Kupta's voice swelled with anger as he stood up. The veins in his forehead pulsed and his eyes bored through the stoic officer who sat unyielding gazing blandly at the ships doctor.

Miller crossed his arms over his narrow chest and said, "Doctor, there is no need for such emotional outbursts," he said, his thick voice as dry as the Mojave Desert.

Kupta turned to face Allen using his hands as wands to emphasize his point. "I'm telling you, Hanson, there's no reasoning with the man. He just doesn't get it."

"Doctor, as you yourself have pointed out on numerous occasions I am not a *man*, and I assure you I do *get it*."

Allen watched the interaction between his two senior officers with a half smile on his lips.

"Okay, gentlemen I think that's enough. Doc, sit down."

Kupta reluctantly sat down in his chair again a look of frustration on his pale face. He stared at the first officer his eyes burning with pent up emotion.

Allen frowned. "I gather someone has solicited a promise from you not to tell me why Amstead was transferred. Naturally, as a Regilusian you must honor this request and keep this information even from me, your commanding officer. Am I correct, Mr. Miller?"

"You are, sir," said Miller.

Allen nodded slowly and studied the science officer's narrow features. "So given that you cannot tell me why Yeoman Amstead was transferred, Mr. Miller I suggest Yeoman Amstead herself requested the transfer."

Kupta's expression changed to shock. "What? Now Hanson I'm sorry but that doesn't make sense. Why would Kelly leave her friends without saying anything?"

"I don't know, Doc, but I plan to find out." Miller's cool eyes watched Allen as he again hit the com button.

"Bell, hail the *Wilson's Folly* and give Captain Jones my warm regards." Jones was an old freighter captain with heavy jowls, and a taste for brandy that rivaled Dr. Kupta's. But Strom Jones was also a man with scruples beyond question.

The red cheeked image of Strom Jones shimmered to life on Allen's viewer. His appearance suggested he'd just enjoyed a taste from his brandy supply. A freighter traveling at level two star driver was more like a pleasure cruise. For the odd passenger they carried it pretty much was just that.

"Hello, Strom it's Hanson Allen." Allen smiled warmly at the man with the fringe of gray hair that ran around his bald cranium like a halo.

Strom's wide face broke into a white toothy smile. "Hanson Allen, while I live and breath. To what do I owe the honor of this call?"

"I was wondering if you still had that passenger aboard you picked up at space station Alpha 7, a blonde woman, mid-twenties."

Strom's suggestive chuckle made Allen wince inside but outwardly he remained the very image of friendly warmth. "Oh, yes that beauty is still aboard. She's been in her cabin for the last two days. Headed for Earth she says. Why Hanson?"

"I need to speak with her."

Strom shook his massive head. "Sorry, Hanson, but she left strict instructions not to be disturbed for the duration of the voyage. I don't ever violate a client's privacy, not for anyone. Not even a mighty ship captain like yourself."

Allen knew it was useless to argue with Strom so he decided to let it go, for now. He shrugged and said, "I understand, my friend. If at some point she comes out of her cabin will you inform her I wish to speak with her?"

Strom nodded with a brief smile on his lips. "Of course. Jones out." The viewer went dark instantly, almost as dark as Allen's mood.

He was getting no where fast. His first officer refused to divulge what he knew, and now Amstead refused to speak with anyone.

What was so damn secret? A cloud of remorse seemed to hang in the air. Maybe she'd left because…no, that couldn't be it.

***

Two hours later Allen's eyes fluttered open his slumber interrupted by the communication whistle once again, and a soft voice bringing him once again into the world of the living.

Kupta had been right he did need sleep. His body felt as if it weighed twice its normal weight as he managed to sit up on his bunk and drop his lean legs over the side.

He rubbed his eyes to clear his bleary vision and then stepped onto the carpet and padded over to his desk. He punched the com button with his thumb.

"Allen here."

"Sir, I have Yeoman Amstead for you."

The weariness in his body left him and he felt more alert than he'd felt in days. *Kelly?* "Thank you, lieutenant, put her through."

The viewer shimmered and the image of Kelly Amstead appeared on the viewer screen.

She wore her hair loose about her shoulders the blonde hair, the color of shimmering straw, cascaded over her purple uniform jumper. Her blue eyes sparkled when she saw him and a brief smile crossed her lips.

"Captain," she said her voice bright and cheery.

"Yeoman Amstead, I'm so glad you called me back. We have something we need to discuss."

She lowered her eyes and her ivory cheeks flushed red. "Yes, sir. I'm very sorry to have caused you any trouble. I just didn't think…"

"That's what I'm afraid of, yeoman. You should have thought this through a title more before you just up and left my ship." Allen struggled to keep the bitterness from his voice.

Her eyes again made contact with his. "Yes, sir, you're quite correct. I told Mr. Miller, and I made him promise not to tell anyone…. I'm embarrassed….sir."

Allen's features registered his surprise. "Embarrassed about what, Kel…yeoman?" Allen felt the heat rising in his cheeks now.

"Well, sir, it's kind of a surprise. I plan to go back to the academy and study to be a communications specialist." Kelly's voice rose in excitement as she spoke.

"Bell and I have been talking about my finding a field of expertise for some time, and when the captain's yeoman program was cancelled I thought the timing was a sign for me to take the leap."

She smiled briefly then dropped her eyes to the floor.

Allen felt his heart sink. How could he have been so blind? This wasn't about him at all. It was about Kelly and her career.

"And when did you plan to tell the crew of my ship?" said Allen.

"When I was accepted into the program," said Amstead.

Allen nodded slowly. "Well, yeoman, then you did the right thing." Allen frowned. "Would it be alright if I told the crew, before you get to the academy? I would, of course send along my recommendations to the acceptance board."

Kelly smiled, her pearl white teeth showing and her eyes sparkled. "Yes, sir, that would be wonderful. I know I've upset everyone there. I'm truly sorry."

Allen sighed. "It's alright, Amstead. I'll handle things at this end."

"And, sir, I just want to say it was a real honor serving with you."

Allen smiled. "Amstead out." The viewer went dark before he could say anything more.

Allen thumbed the communication button. "Allen to bridge."

"Bell here, sir," came the immediate reply. Bell's finger must've been hovering over the switch for his com. He smiled to himself.

"Bell, I'm going to have a shower and a shave then I'll be up. Tell the crew that I'll be making a ship wide announcement when I arrive."

"Yes, sir."

***

Feeling refreshed after his nap, and the shower and shave, and dressed his usual uniform tunic, Hanson Allen walked onto the bridge of the *Earth's Daughter* feeling like a new man.

Miller immediately vacated the center chair and moved to his usual seat at the science station. Allen walked to his chair feeling the eyes of the bridge crew on him as he sat down.

He paused to offer a glance to Bell. He nodded his head slightly and she smiled back.

He then turned and faced the forward viewer and the blackness of star specked space that lay before them.

Allen hit the com button on his chair arm. He'd been thinking about what to say while he was in the shower and then while he shaved.

"Captain to crew. As you know Yeoman Amstead was transferred off this ship a few days ago. Amstead is a good friend to many of you and her sudden departure I know has caused concern among many of you." Allen paused.

"Yeoman Amstead has enrolled in Fleet Academy to become a communications specialist. She did this of her own volition and I can assure all of you her departure was not out of disrespect or malice toward this crew. In fact, she has assured me she was embarrassed to have caused any such feelings."

Allen swiveled his chair to lock eyes with his dark skinned communications officer.

"Kelly wishes me to pass along that it was an honor serving with you all, and that she hopes to serve with many of you again in the future. Captain out."

Allen saw the mist gather at the edges of Bell's eyes until she finally turned away to face her com board.

Just then Kupta walked through the lift doors and hurried to stand beside his chair. His voice was a whisper as he said, "Did she really say all that?"

Allen smiled and nodded. Suddenly he felt a presence beside him and Miller was standing beside his chair opposite doctor Kupta. His thin arms were locked behind his back. Kupta frowned and glared at Miller.

"This is your fault, Miller. You should have told us." Kupta pointed one finger at the Regilusian. Miller's right eyebrow climbed his forehead.

"As you know, doctor, that would have been impossible."

"Well, that's where you people could learn a few things from humanity...." Kupta fumed and blustered as he launched into one his vain attempts to humanize the Regilusian officer.

Allen smiled as he watched his two senior officers in their verbal tussle. He'd let them go on for a while this time.

He thought about Kelly Amstead and her secret. She was a fine person...a fine woman.

He had secrets of his own, which he wasn't about to share with anyone. Not even his two most valued friends in the universe.

Tales From Space

The Family Line

September 15, 2389 in orbit around Telus II

Paul Bellamo sat in the darkness his cabin aboard the Explorer Ship *Nastrodomo*. His skin was cold as ice, and his heart beat rapidly in his chest.

They were gone forever. And nothing would ever bring them back. He stroked the family photo album gently with the long fingers of his right hand. Theirs was a famous line that extended across the centuries making a difference.

It was so unfair.

October 21, 1805 off the south-west coast of Spain, just west of Cape Trafalgar

Tales From Space

Raul Bellamo stood on the sloping forecastle of the French first rate *Redoubtable* struggling to maintain his balance. His eyes and throat stung from the thick, acrid smoke that swirled about him. His once splendid blue uniform was dark with sweat, soot and blood. His clean shaven pale face was marred with his own blood, owing to the shrapnel that has so recently grazed his left ear.

In his left hand he held his saber at the ready, while a primed musket was gripped in his right. Intense sky blue eyes bled with tears due to the acrid smoke as he attempted to orient himself for the inevitable onslaught of the English marines. They were certainly somewhere within the thick cloud of swirling smoke.

Redoubtable, the pride of the French fleet had been slowed by a full barrage of the one hundred twelve cannons launched at them from Admiral Nelson's flag ship, *HMS Victory*. Her sails shredded, her hull pocketed with cannon balls the once mighty three-decked French vessel threatened to wallow, capsize and sink below the heaving seas off Trafalgar.

Bellamo was a junior officer on this, Admiral Villenuve's flag ship. He realized now that the effort to break free of the English blockade had been seriously stymied. The Emperor's plan was lost.

Unlike the professionals of the French fleet their Spanish allies were reluctant sailors. It was doubtful the press gang crews of the Spanish fleet would be much use against the seasoned veterans of the English navy.

Bellamo stumbled across the deck as he wiped the tears that fogged his vision with the sleeve of his uniform tunic. He climbed the short grouping of four stairs that led to the quarterdeck from the now badly listing main deck. The ship creaked loudly in his ears.

"I hope she holds together," he murmured, as he stepped over fallen seamen, some with missing arms or legs.

Parts of the oak deck were slick with blood so he had to weave his way through his fallen ship mates without falling. He'd seen so much death in his short life that the grisly scene had little affect on him. Instead the sight of the dead or dying sailors only incited a heightened sense of rage deep within his belly.

Moans of the dying men echoed through the blanket of dark fog that was like a funeral shroud for the once mighty French fleet.

Finally, the black-gray smoke cleared enough for Bellamo to see the white capped sea beyond. There, with flags waving in the breeze, its tall sails full with wind, its bow rising and falling as it split the green waters of the bay with white foam, was the pride of the English navy bearing down on their crippled vessel now heavy with excess water.

Bellamo knew they were about to be boarded, and unless he could locate some able bodied men to repel the enemy the ship was lost.

He looked around until he spotted, Robby, the ships mate, laying beside a water barrel. His eyes were open but the man was staring at infinity. The left side of his narrow face was covered with dried blood, his white beard peppered with bloody splatter.

Bellamo shook his head at the pitiful site of his old friend lost to him forever.

He moved to the aft section of the deck until the found a nest of wounded seamen. They were alive, huddled in small groups, their arms and legs tied with makeshift tourniquets. Good, this meant the ships surgeon was still alive.

He quickly located Dr. Gillespie who frantically moved amongst the wounded men tending as best he could to their traumatic wounds. Bellamo slipped the musket into the waist band of his trousers, and then replaced his saber in the scabbard dangling from the left side of his waist.

"Doctor, I need your help." Bellamo's voice sounded scratchy in his own ears. No doubt dry due to the smoke he'd inhaled.

Dr. Gillespie turned to gaze at Bellamo with hollow hazel eyes and a bland expression on his grime smudged features. His shoulder length blond hair, streaked with gray, which was normally tied in a neat pony tail, flew about his wide head in a nest of stray fibers. He acknowledged the junior officer with a slight nod of his head, and a heavy sigh. The sound sent a shudder through Bellamo. It was the most world weary noise he'd ever heard.

The doctor stood slowly and Bellamo saw he held a dark stained wooden bowl filed with bloody water. His torn white shirt was also stained with dark red blotches.

"Mister Bellamo, there is very little I can do for you or anyone else on this ship."

"I need men. We are about to be boarded…"

The surgeons eyes narrowed and his full lips became a terse line. "Then perhaps we should raise the white flag. We're in no shape to fight. And the captain is dead."

Bellamo's heart sank with this news. *The Admiral….?*

"And what of Admiral Villeneuve?"

Gillespie shook his head. "Alive. Barely. Sharp shooters."

Bellamo knew ships on both sides carried sharp shooters who sat in the ships rigging. Their orders were to decapitate the officers of an enemy vessel in order to leave them leaderless. He knew he was now in charge. And with a

British ship of the line in full battle sail bearing down on them he also knew he had only minutes to mount a defense.

"Come with me, Doctor," he said briskly his tone and intense gaze daring the older man to refuse his order. The doctor nodded and followed as they headed for the quarterdeck where the ships wheel stood. The smoke was much lighter here so the sun washed blue sky was again visible.

Black tipped gulls cried overhead as they swooped and dived seemingly oblivious to the deadly battle taking place on the seas beneath them.

The odor of smoke cleared Bellamo's lungs to be replaced by the familiar smells of the sea, wind and salt that had first enticed him to join the navy.

When the two men reached the ships wheel Bellamo saw the dark skinned sailor, who he'd last seen steering the massive war ship, hanging limply from the spokes of the ships wheel. Bellamo rushed to the man's side only to see that the back of his skull was missing, having been blown away by an iron ball. Without hesitation Bellamo pushed the corpse to the deck then turned to face the ships doctor.

"You will steer us away from that ship." He nodded toward the three massed English ship that rode the waves speeding toward them.

The doctor's eyes went wide with fear and his face paled as he spotted the English Navy ensign fluttering from the mast. The ship was very near now, and they could clearly see the red coats of the marines their muskets at the ready eager to board the helpless French vessel.

Bellamo glanced upward to the heavy rigging of the *Redoubtable* and spotted two sharp shooters hanging from the rigging, their muskets pointed at the officers gathered on the English fore castle. They were almost in range.

The English will pay for the deaths they've caused.

His breath caught in his throat and his mouth dried as he recognized one British officer's regal bearing. The man was an important target that he hoped the French sharp shooters would also recognize.

He looked around for anything that might help them thwart the enemy, while Dr. Gillespie took control of the ships wheel. Bellamo felt the deck move beneath his feet as Gillespie spun hard in an attempt to steer their vessel away of the onrushing enemy ship.

Finally he spotted the stubby cannonade strapped in place with heavy twisted rope set below the horseshoe shaped rail at the rear of the *dunette* above him. A dead crewman lay on the deck below the gun; the still smoldering wick in his left hand had left its mark on the wooden planks.

Bellamo allowed himself a small smile and rushed up the short flight of steps to the gun.

He checked and sure enough it was primed, loaded and ready to fire. He glanced down at the dead sailor and silently thanked the man for saving the ship.

A glowing steel pot sat in the deck against the bottom rail where the wicks were kept to fire the guns. He picked one, then adjusted the gun to aim at the bow of the enemy ship as she swept toward them pushing boiling white foam ahead of her.

Just as it appeared they would catch the slower French vessel Bellamo fired. The shot was loud and a round iron ball flew from the barrel. It struck where the English marines stood and scattered them like wheat before the scythe.

Bellamo could see the English officers behind them begin to shout orders, and the one who was Bellamo's intended target moved quickly forward exposing himself to the French sharp shooters.

Bellamo heard a crack of a musket being fired from somewhere over his head followed by the report of another that echoed from the direction of the English vessel.

Bellamo felt a sudden, painful blow to his chest that pushed him backward and he fell to the deck.

He heard the doctor cry out as the surgeon rushed to his side. Bellamo's mouth filled with the taste of coppery blood. The doctor managed to lift him with one arm behind his back.

Bellamo felt weak and suddenly very cold. "Did we get him?"

"Who?"

"Nelson…" His eyes glazed over and the sunlit world began to slip into a deep, dark abyss.

"Yes. We got him," said the doctor, unsure in fact if this were true.

A soft smile crossed Bellamo's pained features. With one hand he managed to motion for the doctor to move closer to his lips. "Tell Marie and my precious Emil I love them…" he whispered.

His eyes closed and his body went limp. His last thought as the blackness took him was that the Bellamo family line would continue.

January 5, 2036 Stockholm, Sweden

Dr. Jean Bellamo gazed at the message dumbfounded. How could this be? Dr. Sloan's life threatened? That didn't make sense.

"No, this has to be a mistake," he shook his head to emphasize his point. His mouth was suddenly dry as if the coffee he'd just had had taken every ounce of moisture with it. He removed his wire rimmed spectacles from his hawk like nose and rubbed his pale blue eyes with long craggy fingers.

"Dr. Sloan is a physicist not a politician. Why would anyone want to harm him?" Bellamo opened his eyes and stared at the round face of the bald headed Swedish police detective. The detective's cool blue eyes gazed back at him.

Detective Olafsson was only doing his job, but it was all such nonsense. No sane person threatens the life of a scientist. Not on the eve of the Nobel Prize presentations, unless..... A thought crossed his mind and his eyes hardened.

"I thought we were rid of those damned warlords," he said his voice tainted with deep strain of contempt. It was generally believed those power-mad genetic experiments gone awry had been purged from the surface of the planet over two decades ago. At least that's what most people believed. Bellamo wasn't so sure. Millions had died to rid the world of that corruption of science.

Maybe some of their fanatical followers were attempting to revive those dark times. After all Dr. Sloan's phase technology would make war a kinder, gentler pursuit and there were some fanatics who didn't wish the status quo to be disturbed. Sloan's genius would create a benevolent technology that would end bloody, painful death was not natural they argued. Ignorance was still humankind's chief curse.

"We don't know who's behind this, Dr. Bellamo," said Olafsson with a shrug of his wide shoulders. "We've tested the note in every way we can think of and nothing. We were hoping you might be able to tell us something. How long have you known Dr. Sloan?"

Bellamo smirked. "Albert and I worked together at Berkley." Bellamo placed the note on the faux pine hotel room table as he sat down heavily in the faux leather chair next to the table. Olafsson sat across from him his sky blue eyes intent on Bellamo's every word. "Not exactly together mind you. Albert worked on his physics projects while I'm a chemist."

Olafsson nodded silently as he pulled out his data pad and placed it flat on the table with a barely audible click. He keyed as he asked questions and carefully recorded each response. Bellamo was impressed. Bright man this police officer.

"What are you receiving your award for, doctor? If I may ask."

Bellamo smiled and his eyes sparkled. "Transparent steel." The detective gazed at him with one eyebrow going slightly upward. Bellamo chuckled.

"It's based upon a formula I received from a glass manufacturer in New York some years ago. The man who gave it to me said he'd tried to make it work, but had been unsuccessful. He said two Scottish engineers sold him the formula for sheets of glass." Bellamo smirked. "Not that I believed him naturally. Many of these engineer types attempt new formulas using diverted funds from within their own company. This one failed to produce viable results so he gave it to me."

Bellamo paused again and regarded the detective with a stern expression. "What does any of this have to do with the threat to Albert?"

Olafsson shook his head and shrugged. "Nothing really. It's just that most suspects are often nervous and tend to be closed mouthed when ever I come along."

Bellamo eased back in his chair and unconsciously folded one long leg over the other.

"I don't know whether to treat that as a compliment or be frightened to death."

It was the detective's turn to laugh.

"Sorry, doctor. It's just that we need to interview everyone attending the awards tomorrow and I've just eliminated you from my suspects list." Olafsson slipped his data pad into the inside pocket of his gray suit jacket. "Is there anything else you'd like to add before I leave you?"

"Do you know a restaurant nearby that serves good scampi?"

After the detective had left, not without suggesting the hotel's restaurant for dinner, saying it was the finest in Stockholm; Bellamo stepped into the adjoining bedroom in his suite to dress for dinner.

As was his habit he donned his tanned cotton golf slacks and a canary yellow open necked casual shirt. He slipped into his brown leather slip-ons to finish his ensemble for the evening.

The *Royale's* casino was supposed to be very good, or so some of his associates had told him on the flight from America. Not that he gambled a great deal but he did so enjoy the mental gymnastics inherent in a good game of poker.

As he left his room he swiped the lock with the card they'd given him when he'd checked in earlier in the day then set the voice activated lock. The card would enable the main system at the front desk to keep track of who and how often the room was entered. The voice lock meant only he could enter the room other than hotel staff that needed to. Ever since the Ripson murders five years ago hotel security was a high priority. He shook his head sadly every time he thought about those poor women killed while they slept.

Tales From Space

He walked the short carpeted hallway until he reached the bank of elevators.

One arrived within a few seconds of his pressing the down button. The doors opened and he was surprised to see Albert Sloan's smiling face staring back at him.

"Albert! What a pleasant surprise," Bellamo said as he entered. The elevator doors slid shut behind him and immediately began to move downward. Though there was very little sensation of movement within the car.

Bellamo gripped Albert's ebony hand in his and shook it warmly. For his part Albert placed one hand behind Bellamo's back as they shook hands.

"Peter," said Sloan (Albert always used the American pronunciation of Bellamo's name rather than the French. It was a private joke between the two men.) "It's nice to see you too. Where're you headed?"

"Thought I might try a little lady luck then catch a bite to eat. You?"

Albert chuckled as the let go of Bellamo's hand. "As I recall, Peter, you play a mean hand of poker." Bellamo grinned and nodded.

"Me? I love the slots. Doris and I used to make our yearly trek to Vegas just to play 'em."

Doris Sloan had passed away a year after being diagnosed with cancer. She'd been Albert's wife and best friend for over forty years. Too bad she hadn't lived to see his greatest success.

Bellamo had lost his wife at about the same time in a car accident. The two men had many things in common except Albert and Doris had never had any children while he and Simone had two sons and a daughter. Unlike the Sloan's the Bellamo family line would continue.

"You want to meet for dinner in a couple of hours?" said Bellamo.

Tales From Space

Albert nodded as the car arrived at the lobby level and the doors opened.

The two men parted company with grins on their faces each headed to a different part of the casino complex.

At exactly two hours Bellamo asked the dealer to cash him out as he rose from the card table. Poor Mr. Shipley to his left looked positively ecstatic that Bellamo was leaving.

Of course, Mr. Shipley's stack of chips was considerably reduced in the second hour of Bellamo being at this table. Little did Mr. Shipley know that he'd been up against one of the keenest poker minds of the twenty-first century. Bellamo had seen Mr. Shipley's tells after three hands and had waited to lay his trap in the last two hands.

He'd managed to make a few dollars and felt generally pleased with this evening thus far.

He took the chips to the cashier window and afterward headed for the slots to find Albert.

He strolled past machines with names like Brain Surgeon, Rocket Scientist, and Math Genius. Obviously casino management had recently changed their lineup of slots because the slot machines were supposedly designed to appeal to the Nobel Prize candidates staying at the hotel.

Bellamo smirked. *Inane, positively inane.*

As he rounded a bank of machines he spotted Albert his gazed fixed on the row of numbers on one of the math based dollar slots.

Bellamo glanced around and saw a man who looked out of place. He wore Bermuda shorts and a straw hat. Not one of those wide brimmed ones, but one of those fedora types. Dark sun glasses covered his eyes and he seemed focused on Albert's back as he walked briskly toward the physicist.

Tales From Space

Bellamo felt a rush of adrenalin as he realized immediately something was very wrong. It all seemed like some slow motion movie as the man drew nearer to Albert he reached behind him and drew a pistol from the small of his back hidden underneath the gaudy orange and red Hawaiian shirt he wore.

Bellamo increased his pace until he was running with arms flailing. His shouts of alarm drowned out by the sounds of the slot machines ringing and the blending of voices that blocked every sound. He hadn't noticed until now that the casino was crowded with tourists.

"Gun!" he shouted as loud as he could. He felt his heart pounding against his chest and his mouth was dry now as fear gripped him.

The man kept moving toward Albert his sunglasses fixed on his intended target. He was almost in range as the barrel of the gun was slowly but surely coming up to level. Albert had seconds to live.

Bellamo picked up his pace until he was so close to the killer he imagined he could smell his cheap aftershave. To cover the last leg of his journey Bellamo left his feet like a runner sliding for home. Just as the killer's gun came level Bellamo hit him in a full body tackle his arms wide as he gripped the stout man about his mid section.

Air rushed from both their lungs as he hit the man and then they were both on the gray and blue carpet of the casino. Bellamo felt a twinge of pain in his lower back as he wrestled with the gunman.

Suddenly there was a loud bang. Then another.

The would-be killers sunglasses had fallen off in the struggle and Bellamo could see the surprise that registered in his brown eyes. The man jerked then went limp in his arms and Bellamo took procession of the gun.

He heard a voice say, "Drop it."

Bellamo let go of the gun which fell to the carpet with a dull thud.

"Well, well if it isn't, Dr. Bellamo."

Bellamo glanced over his shoulder and saw Detective Olafsson with a wide grin pasted to his face, his service revolver out stretched in his hands aimed at the gunman who lay face down on the rug. There was a growing pool of blood that reeked of iron as the life drained from the would-be killers body.

"Thanks for the help, doc. You distracted him long enough for me to get him. I guess there's a lot more to you than a Nobel Prize winning egg head."

Bellamo closed his eyes and rolled flat on his back his long, lean arms stretched out to his sides.

Tales From Space

I guess so, he thought, then promptly fainted.

Tales From Space

July 7, 2189 Mars Dome No. 2

Henri Bellamo gazed at the digital photos with tired eyes. He sighed heavily and ran one pale hand over his smooth hairless scalp. Like his father before him he'd lost the majority of his hair before the age of thirty-five.

Seven dead women in seven days and him with no leads. Damn this was the worst case of mass murder in colonization history and he had nothing to go on.

Bellamo's job was to keep the peace in Mars Dome Three, the so called *Euro Dome*. He was ill equipped to handle what had been happening over the past week. The rapidity of the murders, and the single mindedness of it all, caught him and his lone constable completely off guard.

When he'd accepted the job as Chief Constable the recruiter from the United Earth Space Agency told him the assignment would be a cake walk. Sure the licensed brothels tended to work on the finest of legal tight ropes but they were legal.

Until this mess began Mars was a quiet post. A few drunken brawls and kids stealing gum. Nothing they couldn't handle.

Though the victims so far had all been brothel workers he still worried about Yvette and his son LaRue's safety. The miners who worked the asteroid fields had all been located and interviewed. Still nothing. No leads of any kind. It was as if the killer were a ghost.

Henri shook his head to remove such superstitious nonsense from his mind. He lifted his cup of coffee to his lips and nearly gagged when he took a sip into his mouth and realized it had grown cold some time ago. He swallowed the milky, sweet mixture and winced.

He placed the cup on the surface of his transparent steel desk then punched the white com button on the communicator built into the surface of the desk. The light next to the com unit came on indicating the voice mechanism was on.

"Sylvie, is there fresh coffee out there?"

A lilting, slightly accented voice responded. "Oui, Henri." Sylvie was always in a good mood. His mood on the other hand was as dark and as foul as this coffee.

"Thank you." He thumbed the button again to close the link and the light winked out.

He rose from behind his desk and felt his muscles in his lean body protesting his every move. His gray UESA uniform jumper felt tighter than usual. He decided he needed more exercise.

Martian gravity was different from Earth's, or so the doctors had warned him. When they'd arrived with the first colonists two years ago the medical corps cautioned them that daily exercise was needed to counter the loss of bone mass in a lower gravity environment such as Mars.

In a hundred years or so the planet wide reengineering would make Mars more Earth normal. But until that time Martian residents needed to follow the strict regimes inherent in adapting to their new environment.

He moved across the carpeted floor of his office past the brown leather couch that sat against one wall and the potted palm sting next to it that he'd grown from seedlings brought from Earth. The doors to the outer office opened with a soft swoosh moving the recycled air as they parted to allow him to exit.

Sylvie sat smiling behind her desk as he entered the lobby her dark flowing curls and pale porcelain skin glowed with health. Her dark eyes were fixed on her boss. He crossed to the coffee machine to the left of where she sat and began to fix himself a fresh cup.

"You know, Henri you shouldn't put milk and sugar in your coffee. It's not good for you," she said.

Like his wife, Yvette the next thing she'd be suggesting is he drink that horrid Earl Grey she loved so much, instead of his beloved coffee.

As Bellamo lifted the cup toward his lips he said, "And you should always speak Earth standard in the office." He was of course referring to her use of French when she responded to his question over the intercom. The UESA preferred its employees to stick to Earth standard for all official duties.

Bellamo, his nostrils filled with the scent of sweet fresh coffee turned to face his loyal assistant who wore a mischievous smile as flashing eyes met his gaze. He smiled in return then without saying another word walked back into his office the doors sliding shut behind him. Her dark eyes followed him and a frown creased her forehead as the doors slid shut cutting him off from her view.

Once back behind his desk Bellamo hit the com button again. "Signal Blake I wish to see him in my office right away." Sylvie acknowledged his request then closed the link.

Maybe I was a little hard on her. He resolved he'd make it up to her later. Maybe buy her dinner.

Blake Noseworthy was Bellamo's second in command. In fact Blake was his only command, but a good man and someone Bellamo trusted.

While he waited for Blake to arrive Bellamo again pulled up the crime scene reports and digi-photos. The vital clue had to be in here somewhere.

The UESA detectives and forensic specialists wouldn't arrive for another day. By that time he hoped to have something more for them that the wisps of smoke he'd managed to collect thus far.

The doors to his office swooshed open and the blond blue eyed giant with the square jaw of Blake Noseworthy rushed through the doors. He stopped in front of his boss' desk and stood casually his meaty hands at his sides.

"Yes sir?" he said in his characteristic deep voice.

Bellamo regarded Blake with one eyebrow raised. "Sit down, Blake."

Bellamo nodded to the forest green cloth covered chair that sat opposite him across the desk. Blake immediately sat down his eyes focused on Bellamo's. Since they'd began to work together the two men had become like brothers. There were times Bellamo was certain Blake could actually read his thoughts.

"I have a plan," Bellamo began. "We're going to end this thing tonight."

Blake nodded grimly his eyes as hard as diamond and his jaw line tight.

***

Five hours later Sylvie sat shivering in a booth at Le Café, a coffee house across from the row of brothels that ran down Churchill Street in sector B, the area known as the red light district.

The place was deserted except for a greasy haired waiter, the cook in the back and Sylvie. She sat with a cup of Earl Grey in front of her keeping her coat pulled up around her neck. She cast a wary gaze on the street outside.

A few of the brothel workers were talking with some miners who'd just left one of the bars down the street.

Sylvie cringed inside. *How did I ever let Henri talk me into this? He said I'd be perfectly safe.* "Yeah right," she muttered.

"Yeah?" It was the oil-slick haired waiter with the fox like face and the beady eyes. He stood over her with an empty black plastic serving tray held aloft in his right hand.

"Sorry," she said. "I'm waiting for someone."

The waiter smirked. "Yeah, sure you are, lady." He shrugged. "If you need anything I'll be over at the counter watching the Wimbledon matches."

She nodded. "Okay, thanks." She smiled weakly. He grimaced and walked away leaving her alone once again.

She glanced at her digital watch and saw that it was time. The murders had all occurred at about the same time of night.

The street workers had been recruiting customers in the street when they disappeared.

Tales From Space

The street hadn't been deserted each time there was a murder. Yet no one had seen anything. It was as if the victims just vanished.

The bodies turned up later in one of several streets that led to this area of the dome. The victims had been horribly mutilated and disemboweled.

As she stood in the dim light watching the pedestrian traffic go by some of the miners winked at her, but with the look she made it very clear she wasn't interested. Nothing more happened for some time.

"Where are you, Henri?" she whispered under her breath.

A familiar voice interrupted her thoughts. "Hello, Sylvie." It was Blake.

"Oh, Blake it's you." She whirled and faced the big man.

He grinned easily and wrapped his long muscular arms around her. "You okay?" he said. "You're shivering."

"I think I've had enough for one night," she breathed as they parted. "I should never have told Henri I would do this. I'm scared out of my wits."

Blake nodded. "I understand. Can I walk you home?"

"Yes, please, if you don't mind?"

Blake nodded a grin on his face as he held out one arm. "Come along, my lady."

She giggled and a brief smile crossed her lips. "Ah, sir knight, such gallantry. I accept."

With a flourish that harkened back to the days of chivalry they walked arm in arm toward one of the streets that led them away from the sector B toward sector G where Sylvie resided.

Once sector B was behind them Sylvie let go and they walked along in silence for several seconds until Blake said, "You like the boss don't you?"

"Why whatever gave you that idea?" Sylvie could feel the heat rise in her face.

"Oh, I don't know. It could be the way you look at him, or the trace of drool that runs down your chin wherever you're around him."

She slapped his left arm playfully. "Oh, I do not."

"Yes, you do. You're in love with him aren't you?" He said it with enough conviction that it caused her to stop and turn to face him.

"If I was what business would it be of yours?" She surprised herself with the forcefulness of her response. She was angry.

He shrugged. "None, of course, it's just that...."

"What?"

"Well, if it's true I'm going to have to kill you."

Sylvie heart skipped a beat and her mouth went dry. "You're what?"

"Kill you," he repeated. He reached behind his back and pulled out a large curved blade that glistened in the low light of the artificial Martian night.

She stepped back, hands raised to a defensive position, a scream choked in her throat. She was too afraid to scream.

This isn't right. Blake's one of the good guys.

He moved with the reflexes of a cat and was swiftly upon her. She could smell the roast beef he'd had for dinner still lingering on his breath. She felt a slight pinch in her stomach as his meaty left hand pulled her slim body toward him and impaled her with the knife.

Suddenly her hearing was filled with the sound of a laser weapon being fired. She felt Blake jerk against her then they fell as one with his full weight on top of her, the knife pressing deeper into her flesh.

Finally a gargled scream escaped her lips only to be muffled by his body as they hit the tiled floor of the street.

She couldn't breath. She was dying and she knew it.

Hands pulled Blake away from her and she could once again manage a breath. Her lungs burned. The pain from the knife was increasing. Her toes and fingers felt colder than they'd ever felt before. Not even Minnesota winters were this cold.

A familiar face bent over hers. Through foggy vision she recognized Henri's handsome features. "Sylvie, I'm so sorry. I had no idea…" His voice trailed off.

She managed to raise one weak hand to her lips to silence him then motioned for

Bellamo to come closer. He bent over her one ear hovering above her blood-stained full lips.

"I love you, Henri Bellamo. I always have," she whispered. Until she sagged and her eyes closed for the last time as the swirling dark vortex of death took her.

***

Henri Bellamo stood over his assistant's body his heart heavy with regret. She loved him so much she'd sacrificed her life to help him solve the murders.

He moved to Blake and checked for a pulse. Nothing. The man was dead.

Good riddance to him. How could he have been so wrong about him? Maybe he needed to give up this job and return to Earth. He certainly couldn't be a constable anymore, not with Sylvie's blood on his hands.

He resolved to one day tell young LaRue about this day. Maybe there was lesson in this for his son. Then again, maybe not.

Odd thing was the laser weapon had been set on stun not kill. Blake shouldn't be dead yet he was.

There were many odd things about all this. He shrugged his narrow shoulders. The investigators would get to the bottom of it, after all that was their job wasn't it?

A steel gray haired man with the cool dark eyes stood amongst the crowd that had gathered to see what was happening. He gazed at the chief constable with a faint smile on his thin lips. The man turned and walked away headed for the space port. It was time to move on.

September 15, 2389 in orbit around Telus II

Tales From Space

The family line was at an end. His dearly beloved nephew, Robert was the last son of the Bellamo family. The last hope.

Paul recalled the stories papa had told him and his brother, Pierre as they sat round the camp fire. The blanket of stars that washed the summer sky overhead had been a beacon to him even then. And more so than having a family of his own. Pierre took care of the family line for them both. The deadly fire had burned out the family line.

As boys he and his brother reveled in those tales of triumph and tragedy that papa had lain before them. Trafalgar, the Nobel Prize, the Martian colonies…the Bellamo line had been there throughout history. Humankind was better off for having Bellamo's.

Now that was over—

—there would be no more Bellamo family line.

Tales From Space

Big Business

He who's the fattest wins.

The banner running across the poster of the new triple cheesier was the company slogan fifteen year old Peter Pug really hated.

He gazed at the banner fluttering in the gentle breeze hung over the entry doors of the glass tower that ran up seventy stories into the white puffy clouds the weather bureau had created for today.

He paused his hover chair to scratch the roll of fat that hung over the left side of the gravity belt struggling to keep his silver stretch pants above his waist line. The goal was to live up to those important words. He had never felt capable of living up to his mother's expectations never mind the company motto.

Tales From Space

The best burgers and fries made them the second largest fast food company in the galactic franchise wars. Heavenly Sky Burger had somehow never been able to crack the glass ceiling to make it to number one.

Peter floated inside and took the high speed elevator to the executive office on the seventh floor. He entered his mother's office to find her seat in her hover chair behind her expansive plasti-steel desk engrossed in something on her vid screen inset into the smooth desktop.

Without looking up she said, "There you are." Her voice was deep and throaty. "Where have you been?"

"Huh..I've been down in food additives supervising some new…"

"Forget that crap," she said interrupting with a wave of a bloated hand.

"Yesss, mother," he said, his voice trembled as fear ran through his gelatin like frame, which caused him to tremble and jiggle. She was a scary woman, like most people of absolute power. His father was the only person he'd ever known to stand up in the face of her intimidation, and won.

"I've a very important job for you, and this time you'd better not screw it up."

His eyes fixed on the thick pile of the purple and gray carpet that covered the flexi-steel floor of her office. The delicious greasy smells coming from the insta-burger bar against the far wall made his stomach rumble. He hoped she'd let him eat soon.

"Com'on, Peter, let's get something to eat. I'll fill you in on the details." Her tone lightened.

The chair lifted away from the desk then carried her to the food bar by sliding on its four wheeled base. It was the latest automatic model made for the obese woman who had everything. And Trixie Pug, as Chief Operating Officer of HSB, had everything.

The insta-burger deposited a triple cheese burger with a large side of French fries on a white coated metal platter and slid it to the edge of the counter. The smell made Peter's mouth water. He swallowed the extra saliva.

Trixie lifted it from the platter between her well rounded digits.

Peter strode after her with a plate of the new fried chicken. He really wanted his usual burger, but what he wanted most was to please his mother, and she wanted him to try the new product. At least it was deep fried. He stopped his hover chair across the desk from her.

She grimaced at him as she raised the burger to her ample mouth, tore a large bite off and began to chew loudly with her mouth open.

Tales From Space

"Hummpf," she mumbled in between chews, "I have a mission for you. It involves your father."

He stopped in mid-bite of greasy chicken his mouth gapping at her. His father? Sure he was the best FTL scientist in the galaxy, and probably the most responsible for the continued expansion of the HSB, but he also knew his mother detested him.

He insisted on being slim and trim when normal people prided themselves on being as fat as humanly possible. Obesity is in and fat is beautiful, baby. Doctor of Engineering, Herman Pug voted the skinniest guy in the class of 3302 (not an honor) was the black sheep amongst the Pugs.

***

Herman Pug studied the three dimensional schematic image of the engine hovering over his desk.

Tales From Space

Yes, it just might work.

Trixie's quest for power and her efforts to become the number one fast food company were dangerous obsessions as far as he was concerned.

The love he'd once felt for her vanished with the gathering weight and the accompanying cravings for power that propelled her up the corporate ladder.

He recalled fondly the times she joined the HSB marketing department as a junior executive. They'd soon gone their separate ways when the love she'd felt for him was replaced with grease.

These days he put all his energy into his engines. Especially when he wasn't the one paying the bills.

Mickelott, the half moon shaped purple from Marzipan Two. A planet named by some dumb ass pilot from one of the two fast food giants. They were always naming newly discovered planets after some condiment. It made for some down right weird names; Olives, Ketchup and Double-Onions-Raw-or-Fried.

Halo sat quietly on the edge of the table happily slurping on his bowl of green mush. Gary wondered why whoever decided such things hadn't called the aliens planet green mush.

"Mickey, do you really have to make all that noise? I'm trying to work."

The transparent purple slug's front end that Herman concluded long ago was his mouth was not his ass.

"Yeah, well you're interrupting my meal."

The little alien's words shot through his mind. God how he hated telepathy, but the little guy had grown on him ever since he'd found the alien stowed away on one of the automated marketeer FTL ships.

Tales From Space

Herman had been a receiving clerk at the time and his duties included unloading marketeer retiring from deep space marketing missions. He had discovered Mickey dehydrated and starving. He nursed him back health and they'd been best friends ever since.

The bell on the entrance door to the lab buzzed which interrupted his train of thought.

"Come," he said. This single word caused the double doors, visible from his desk, to swoosh as they slid aside.

There stood his son, Peter in his silver gravity suit, his massive stomach sticking out in front of him. His cheeks seemed puffier than when he'd last seen him a year ago, no doubt he'd gained weight since then.

This was unexpected. *Oh, now what?* thought Herman.

Mickey's gossamer wings appeared from the sides of his body. They spread outward and began to flap, making him appear to be some purple alien bird. He lifted off and began to hover in place near the desk.

"Hi, Dad," said Peter. He glanced about his father's lab, his eyes nervous.

"I'm rather busy right now." Herman kept his gaze fixed on the image that rose off the glass surface of his desk. "Holo off."

The image vanished and he sat down heavily in the black executive leather chair behind it.

***

Peter saw Mickey move away until he hovered over the large air couch set against one wall. The dim light made it difficult to see him floating there.

Peter flossed his hover chair purposefully toward the desk. (At least he hoped it appeared purposeful. You could never tell with a hover chair.)

Once he stopped he glanced about the room nervously. The odor of his own perspiration filled the room. Perspiration now flowed off his forehead in rivulets. He reached into a breast pocket of his suit to extract a white towel, which he used to wipe off the excess moisture. He hated when mom sent him down here to speak with dad. They really hated each other. It made him nervous.

"You should lose some weight,' said his father with a deadpan expression.

"Yeah…right." Like *that* would ever happen. And if he did he'd be ostracized by everyone.

His father put his hands in the pockets of his white lab coat and eased back in his chair. "So what do you want?"

"Who says I want anything? Maybe I just dropped by to see my dear old dad?"

"Don't start with the bull, kid."

"Huh... yeah." Peter leaned forward, as much as he was able, his belly didn't allow him much movement. "Listen, could you ask that slug thingy to get out of here so we can talk."

"He's my trusted lab assistant actually, whatever you say to me you say to him."

Peter fidgeted visibly as he struggled with the next words out of his mouth. "Listen, Dad, this isn't easy...

"Your mother needs my help? Right?"

Peter's face flushed and his mouth hung open. His blood shot blue eyes went wide, like a space bug before it hit the windshield of a shuttle craft. He stammered unable to speak.

"She wants my latest engine doesn't she?" His Dad crossed his arms across his chest a move which would have killed Peter had he attempted it. Not that he would ever try. "You can get you're fat butt back to her right now and tell her to forget it."

Tales From Space

Peter struggled to his feet and fled his father's laboratory his hover chair's motor whining under the strain of the sudden increase in speed.

***

Herman could hear the echo of his son's labored breathing as the doors swooshed shut behind him.

"That was a little harsh don't you think?" said Mickey.

"They piss me off. They're all about greed. I'm a scientist damn it, not a profit monger. There's no way in hell I'm giving them another of my inventions. They'll waste it on some hair brained market expansion plan. I'm an explorer at heart."

Herman thought he could hear the little purple roll his eyes, if he'd had any eyes to roll. Mickey didn't approve of Herman's attitude toward his son.

Tales From Space

They'd stayed up late at the nearby poker parlor many a night talking, arguing really, about Peter and his ex-wife. Mickey advocated involvement in his son's life.

Herman said he didn't want any part of the corporate life that Peter and Trixie whole heartedly embraced.

He didn't care about being the fattest, or the greediest. It seemed to him money and fat, and fat and money was all they cared about. He wanted none of those things. As far as she was concerned their lives' were wasted. To him it was sad and reprehensible at the same time.

Build them a newer and faster FTL ship? Trixie had been trying for years to get him to build her one. He frowned and crossed his arms over his chest. Never.

***

Tales From Space

"What do you mean he won't help us? We own his ass."

Peter cowered before his mother. She floated her chair carrying her massive bulk to the food dispenser to order a triple cheese with fries.

He felt pride as he watched her move across the spacious office. She was good and fat. Through the window he watched as many as five automated FTL ships launch from the docking bay doors at once.

The leather over stuffed chair he sat in creaked as he tried to shrink into it. He wanted to disappear, a physical impossibility for a boy with a seventy two inch waist.

"But, Mom…" He was cut short by her glare, her dark eyes bored through him over the sesame seed covered bun of the triple cheeser. His stomach growled as the delectable odor of the cooked meat and cheese wafted over him. He swallowed hard. "I tried…"

"Never mind," she said cutting him off with a fierce snap in her voice. The last bite of burger, secret sauce, and cheese disappeared as Trixie paused to steeple her enormous greasy fingers.

Her beady eyes narrowed. The silence was only being broken by her chewing. "Tell him I want to see him. Tomorrow," she said, after the last large swallow of her burger.

She chuckled to herself. Her rolls of fat, beneath the green and red flowers of her muumuu, waved as if in a strong breeze. With a wave of her corpulent hands she dismissed him.

He struggled out of the chair and adjusted the gravity setting on his chair to retreat as fast as his massive body would allow.

As he neared the exit doors he heard her murmur to herself. "I need to meet with the board this afternoon."

Her sharp laugh followed him to the outer office to be cut off by the doors as they clapped shut with a loud *thunk*.

***

At precisely nine the next morning Herman Pug, accompanied by Mickey who flew over his left shoulder, strode into the spacious office of Trixie Pug, President of Heavenly Sky Burger. Her eyes narrowed as she saw him walk in with his purple slug. She'd turn on the old charm and set it to full.

Trixie's huge face contorted to be equal parts pleasure, apprehension and wariness. Then again it might just be gas. She was well aware her ex-husband didn't usually respond well to summons from her.

Tales From Space

Perhaps her memo stating that the funding for his research was being reduced to zero percent had been the deciding factor after all. They both knew it was an empty threat but the game had to be played. They both knew that HSB needed R&D as much as it needed marketing if they were to remain competitive.

"So," she began then her voice trailed off.

He kept his hands in the pockets of his white lab coat. The awkward silence between them elongated and beads of perspiration began to appear on her forehead.

Framed by the window behind her were a number of auto-ships taking off and one small flitter its navigation lights glowing and blinking pulling a sign behind it. The sign was surrounded by a string of glowing multicolored lights that blinked at regular intervals. In the center of the sign were the words; *He Who's the Fattest Wins.*

He grimaced. A perplexed looked crossed Trixie's face until she glanced behind to see what he was looking at.

"You never approved of what we're trying to do." She said it in a matter of fact manner. Not as a question, but as a statement. He kept staring out the window.

"How can I?" he said. "You're killing the human race."

She spun her chair to face him and a flash of anger crossed features. Her puffy cheeks glowed red as if her skin were on fire. "We are advancing the corporate business plan. Big business is a reality. We're here to stay whether dissidents such as you like it or not."

Herman stiffened and he felt his hands tighten in the pockets of his lab coat. He spoke from between gritted teeth. "I didn't come here to have the same old argument with you, Trix. What do you want?"

Trixie regained her composure and adjusted her bulk in her chair. As she did so her face transformed into a smile, one that was politician like, presidential in a way. She was supposed to go corporate during times like this, and that was one area where she was particularly skilled. Being the second best corporate president in the galaxy had taught her something, if in doubt bullshit.

"Let's not start off in the wrong direction. I have an offer for you."

"One that I can't refuse?" said Gary his voice dripping with sarcasm. Halo chuckled as he floated nearby thoroughly enjoying the action. He loved the interaction of humans. From the corner of his eye Herman looked at the purple and a brief smiled crossed his lips. He then returned a stoic gaze at Trixie.

She smiled broadly. "Of course you can refuse, but I think you will like what I have to offer."

A small control panel appeared from her desk and she pushed a button. A holo-screen dropped down from a five foot slot in the ceiling. The over head lighting system dimmed.

"Cool. Movies," said Mickey drifting over to the couch against the opposite wall. Herman remained in the chair in front of Trixie's desk.

"Where's the popcorn?" said the alien. Trixie glared at Herman who shrugged.

Trixie touched the control panel again and the red and blue Planet Burger logo appeared on the screen in living holo-color. The company theme song began to play again.

The scene immediately shifted to a picture of Trixie sitting behind her desk.

"Hello, I'm Trixie Pug, President of the Heavenly Sky Burger Corporation. I'm speaking to

the board of directors today about our new improved corporate business plan, our most ambitious yet." Trixie's image paused for dramatic effect.

"No, it does not involve a new improved menu, as I'm sure we're all used to." Trixie chuckled as did her likeness on the screen. "I love that joke," said Trixie.

Herman smirked and shook his head.

Trixie's image turned to the camera. "Shortly we will be opening exciting new markets. I'm speaking about a new class of FTL ship that will take us to the Andromeda galaxy. A place where no fast food company has gone before." The faux Trixie raised one meaty arm over her head and her face became bright red.

Her image was replaced by the HSB logo. An announcer's voice, a man who spoke in the style of a man being chased by mad dogs (which maybe he was), came over hidden speakers.

"*This program is copyrighted by the HSB Corporation. No part may be duplicated in part or in whole without the expression written permission of the company. Failure to adhere to this strict company policy will result in an immediate death sentence without benefit of trial.*"

"And the fat lady sings," said Mickey cackling.

The lights came up as the widows once again became clear and the room returned to its original configuration.

Herman removed his hands from his pockets and placed them folded in his lap.

"So," he began slowly," I'll ask again what does *any* of this have to do with me?"

"Isn't it obvious?" said Trixie with a puzzled expression. Anyone could clearly see what they were getting at. Herman, however, shook his head.

"They want to have your new FTL drive. Or they go under," said Mickey who'd risen from the couch his wings spread from his purple slug shaped body allowed him to float as if on he was a butterfly on a gentle breeze.

Trixie pointed at the purple alien. "What he said." She eased back in her chair her arms at her sides a satisfied smiled across her ruddy complexion.

"What's in it for me?" said Herman.

He'd planned this moment for weeks. He knew it was only a matter of time before one of the fast food giants approached him for his know how. He knew he could get his wife to make the best deal of the two biggies. Even though he currently worked for Planet Burger jumping ships wasn't unheard of, not in corporate culture where it was dog eat dog (he suppressed the urge to laugh at this thought).

Tales From Space

He remembered 'ol Marty Smartman, the candy prize pack king, who'd started out in corporate development at Pizza Comet until he'd stolen all the patents for the toys in the kids packs, then set himself up as the exclusive supplier of toys to every fast food company in the known galaxy.

It was something Trix knew as well as he did, maybe even better. No, she wouldn't miss this opportunity. No siree.

He had his eye on a little paradise planet, near the relish worlds of Green Dill and Hamburger Red. This deal would finally give him the money to escape the corporate rat race, and maybe alleviate himself of some familial baggage at the same time.

All he needed to do was play his cards right.

Trixie piggy eyes narrowed until they were mere slits of dark matter. She placed her flabby arms flat on the polished surface of her desk. They spread out like two pools of steaming flesh colored goo.

"How about ten percent?" An eyebrow arched.

He gazed impassively into the slits above Trixie's bulbous cheeks. "Are you joking?"

She smiled. "Somehow I didn't think you'd roll that easy. Okay. What's reasonable?"

She eased back in her chair and gazed at the little purple hovering across the room, its web like wings flapping lazily in the still air.

Herman sensed the fear start deep in his stomach. Butterflies moved. He mentally pushed the feeling down. He smelled the grease coming from her pores. She was nervous, but didn't show it outwardly. It dawned on him that the corporation had a final offer in mind. He decided to go for broke.

"Fifty one percent of what ever profits are realized in the expansion to Andromeda."

Both eyebrows went up. "Since when you become so corporate?" She smiled. "Of course, we can't give you controlling interest." She didn't make a counter offer, so he did.

"I understand, how about five trillion in cash and stock options?" He kept his face free of any expression. This was what he really wanted. The cash would buy him a reliable ship, to get to his new planet, which he would buy, the real estate fees, taxes and with enough spending money left over to retire in comfort for the rest of his days.

"Okay," she said, "deal."

He realized he'd made it too easy, but he'd gotten what he wanted, and so had she.

***

Mickey hovered over his shoulder as Herman watched the new FTL ship slip through the bay doors. Trix was nice enough to let him watch the launch from her office.

She told him *skinnies* weren't allowed on the VIP platform on the hangar deck. Only the beautiful people were allowed. Besides she said the wide angle lenses would most certainly miss one skinny little guy amongst all that beauty.

The ship disappeared in a blinding burst of light as the new engine was engaged. They were on their way to disappear on a long journey.

He smiled.

"How long are they going to be gone?" said Mickey.

"A long time," said Herman as he reached into the pockets of his white lab coat and pulled out two round balls. These were the drive crystals that made the FTL system work. One set got you where you were going, while and another set got you back.

Tales From Space

It was a small detail. One which he'd failed to share with Trixie, or Peter, when they insisted their executive assistants on going on the maiden trip.

He thought maybe they'd start a new fast food company over there? Who knows maybe the Andromedans possessed their own fast food companies. You just never know. Big business was a harsh mistress. The fattest lost this time. The two assistants were never coming back. The trip was one way, a voyage of no return.

Trixie would have to honor their agreement or lose face to the board of directors. he'd proven the new technology. She just hadn't been specific enough. She never said the ship had to return.

Boy, was she gonna be mad at me. He smiled to himself.

He walked away from the window with Mickey close behind. The doors opened and he

Tales From Space

walked out to begin his journey to his new home closer to the freedom he so craved.

About the Author

Russ Crossley writes romance under the name R.G. Hart, mystery under the name R.G. Crossley, and science fiction and fantasy under his own. This year there will be re-issues the romantic comedies, Bachelorette: Zombie Edition and Antique Virgin originally published by Sapphire Blue Publishing, an additional paranormal romantic comedy, Zomopolis, and a new original western romance entitled, The Fire In Their Hearts co-authored with R.S. Meger.

He has sold several short stories that have appeared in anthologies from Pocket Books, St. Matins Press, at Smashwords, and other e-retail sites.

With his wife, romance author R.S. Meger, he owns and operates a small press publishing company, 53rd Street Publishing. The company began in April 2011 and now has over sixty e-book titles and two print titles, with more planned in 2012.

He is a member of SF Canada and the Greater Vancouver Chapter of Romance Writers of America. He is also an alumni of the Oregon Coast Professional Fiction Writers Master Class taught by award winning author/editors,

Tales From Space

Kristine Katherine Rusch and Dean Wesley Smith.
 To find a complete listing of his work check out his website http://www.rghart.com, http://russstory.blogspot.com. Razor's blog can be found at http://razorandedge.blogspot.com
 Feel free to contact him on Facebook or Twitter. He loves to hear from readers

Tales From Space

Other titles by the Author

Titles as R.G. Crossley

Short Stories

Razor and Edge Mysteries
The Kidnapping of Billy Buttons
String of Pearls
Death by Clown
Beggin' For Murder
Ragged Ice
The Grand Central Mystery

Non-Series Mysteries
A Day Without Sunshine
Mirror Image
Dangerous Waters
Cape Disappointment
Boomerang
The Watcher of Wayburn Street
The Apprentice
Drip!
A Beautiful Friendship and The Parrot of Doom
Merry Island
The Christmas Club
Loose Ends

Tales From Space

Anthologies
The Adventures of Razor and Edge: Five Tales From The Quirky Detective Team

Novels
Shear Murder (coming soon)
A Bad Case of Loyalty
The Last Serial Killer

Titles as Russ Crossley

Novels
Attack of the Lushites

Short Stories
Countdown
Shoeless Moe
Round Up At The Burger Bar: The Story of Trixie Pug, Parts 1, 2, 3, 4, 5
Five Minutes
Blossom Queen, Barbarian
The Secret
The Family Line
End of the Flies
With Death You Get the Eggroll
The Penguin Sleeps With The Fishes
Only The Worthy

Tales From Space

Hero For A Day
End of Empire
Strange Bedfellows
Big Business
A Perfect Crime
The Wise Guy and The Pirates
In Search of the Perfect Cup
T.I.N. Men
The Legend of G and the Dragonettes
The Incredible Mr. Fix-It

Presents Anthology Series
Five Tales of Urban Fantasy
Five Tales of Bizarre Detectives
Five Tales of Mystery and Suspense
Five Tales of Weird Fantasy
Spies, Detectives, & Heroes
Tales of Twisted Crime
Five Tales of The Unexpected
Tales From Space

Titles as R.G. Hart

Short Stories
Tikka's Big Day
"My Partner the Zombie" — *Hungry For Your Love*
Anthology (St. Martin's Press)
Big Hairy Deal
One Red Shoe

Tales From Space

A Bad Day in Lunden Texas

Novels
Bachelorette: Zombie Edition - Champagne Books
Antique Virgin
The Fire In Their Hearts with R.S. Meger (coming soon)
Zomopolis (coming soon from 53rd Street Publishing)

CPSIA information can be obtained at www.ICGtesting.com
Printed in the USA
LVOW131929070812

293349LV00022B/323/P